A Note to Readers

While the Bowman and Stevenson families are fictional, many of the situations they find themselves in really happened. On April 4, 1903, huge crowds turned out in St. Paul when President Theodore Roosevelt visited Minneapolis and St. Paul. The president was in the first carriage of a parade that included veterans from the Civil War and the Spanish-American War, as well as members of the Minnesota National Guard.

Automobiles were still very expensive because Henry Ford had not yet invented the assembly line, but telephones were increasingly common—especially in cities. Most cities did not have car dealerships, and cars were ordered from catalogs. They'd take months to arrive by train. Electric cars were popular because they were easier to operate.

Also, it was much easier for immigrants to become U.S. citizens in 1903 than it is now. At the beginning of the twentieth century, large numbers of people were coming to the United States with dreams of starting a better life.

SISTERS IN TIME

Maureen
the Detective

THE AGE OF IMMIGRATION

VEDA BOYD JONES

BARBOUR
PUBLISHING

Maureen
the Detective

For Doc

Cover design by Lookout Design Group, Inc.

Published by Barbour Publishing, Inc., P.O. Box 719, Uhrichsville, Ohio 44683 www.barbourbooks.com

Our mission is to publish and distribute inspirational products offering exceptional value and biblical encouragement to the masses.

ⓔⓒⓟⓐ Member of the
Evangelical Christian
Publishers Association

Printed in the United States of America.
5 4 3 2 1

CONTENTS

CHAPTER 1

Crazy Old Lady Hoag

Maureen O'Callaghan Stevenson saw it first. She knew the minute she saw it that it would change her life in one more way. She didn't know how or why. It was just a feeling, but she didn't know if she could stand one more change.

She and Mark Bowman, a cousin she'd gained when the Stevensons had adopted her two months ago, were down by the creek a few blocks from her house. Mark was skipping rocks a little ways upstream. Maureen had been walking along the bank, searching for flat rocks to throw, when she'd looked across the water and seen something hung up on a huge log. She found a long stick and tried to reach it.

"Maureen!" Mark yelled. "What're you doing?"

"I've found something!" she yelled back. "Come help me."

Mark scurried to her side. "What've you got?"

"I think it's a woman's handbag. It's stuck by that log. See?" She pointed, but he shook his head, and she moved him to her position so he could see better.

"Hmm," he mumbled. "Why don't you go out on that log and get it?"

"Do you want to go out there?" Maureen had fallen off that log into the knee-deep water last summer when she didn't mind getting wet, and her mama had scolded her then. In mid-March there was ice around the banks, and an accidental dipping would be frigid. Besides, she wasn't about to do something that would cause her new adoptive mother to raise her voice. It wasn't that she was scared of Nadine Stevenson—she just didn't want to do anything to upset their new relationship.

"We need a bigger stick," Mark said.

They looked around the area and found a longer one. It could reach the handbag, but it broke off before they could pry the handbag loose.

Trees lined the water's edge. Maureen found a long branch that had been blown down by high winds some time ago. Mark used his pocketknife to whittle off the twigs that stuck out from it so it could be a smooth rod.

"It's frozen in there," Maureen said as he approached the edge of the creek with the branch.

"We'll get it out now." Mark held the branch out in front of him. "Hold on to me." Maureen grabbed his belt, and he leaned way out to poke at the handbag. He slipped, but Maureen's strong grasp kept him out of the water. Only the toe of his boot got wet.

Mark jabbed at the handbag, and ice cracked around it. He hooked the branch through the strap, and it came up with a force that knocked him into Maureen. They both fell to the ground. The purse slid down the slick branch right into Mark's arms.

"Let me see it," Maureen said. "Boys shouldn't look in a lady's handbag."

He gave the small black leather bag to her, and she opened the clasp. Inside were soggy papers that were frozen together in places. Maureen took out the papers and handed the bag back to Mark.

She gently tugged on the edges of the papers, separating a few.

"Ooohh," Mark said excitedly. He stood there with his eyes big and his mouth hanging open.

"Mark? Are you all right?"

"There's money in here. Maybe a hundred dollars!" He held out a clump of frozen bills.

"Where'd you find that?"

"In this inside compartment, under this little flap. We're rich." He pried the money apart and started counting.

"It's not our money," Maureen said. "We might find the name of the owner." She worked at separating the papers. The ink on the top pages had faded and was unreadable.

"Ninety-six dollars," Mark announced. "We found the money. It could belong to anyone in Minneapolis. There are more than two hundred thousand people. We'll never find the owner."

"Men don't carry handbags, so you can cut that number in half." She separated an envelope from the wet papers. "Besides, here's a name. Mrs. Franklin Hoag," Maureen read.

"Not Crazy Old Lady Hoag!" Mark said.

"Don't call her that," Maureen said. She had never met the eccentric woman who lived down the street from her, but she knew all about her. It was actually Mrs. Hoag's property they were on now. Her house fronted close to the street, but her extensive grounds covered several acres—part wooded, part cleared—and the shallow creek flowed through the eastern part of her land.

"My brother told me she doesn't ever leave her house," Mark said.

"That doesn't make her crazy." Maureen had heard the rumors that the old woman had become a recluse since her husband had died two years earlier. That was something Maureen could understand. Her mama had died only three months ago, and there had been times she'd wanted to crawl into a hole and never get out. "We have to take this handbag to her."

"I'm not going to her house," Mark said. "Look for another name. Maybe it doesn't belong to her."

Maureen picked the papers apart and looked at each one. Now that she knew the name she was looking for, she could make out the dim markings as Mrs. Hoag's name.

"It's hers. I'm going to take it back. You can come with me or stay here. That's up to you, but it's the right thing to do." She turned to walk along the creek bank toward the street.

Mark hesitated, and for a moment Maureen thought he wasn't going to follow her, but then he sprang into action.

"All right, I'll go so you don't have to go alone. But we have to be careful. She might attack us."

"Don't be silly. Why would she do that?"

"You never know with crazy people," Mark said.

Maureen ignored his remark and quickened her step. The chill of the day was starting to creep into her bones, and she shivered. "I wonder how she lost her handbag. What would she be doing down by the creek?"

"Maybe it was stolen. Maybe she'll think we stole it."

"Now, why would she be thinking that? Thieves don't return things they've stolen."

Maureen could see the high roof of Mrs. Hoag's house through the bare branches of the nearby trees. The house was huge—a mansion, really. *Mrs. Hoag must be lonely living there all by herself,* she thought.

"Let's cut to the street now," Mark said.

They moved into the wide street and hurried along. Now Maureen could see the front of the house. Round brick columns soared three stories tall, holding up balconies on the second and third floors. It was one of the few homes made of brick, and Maureen's new mother had told her it had been there for nearly sixty years.

It was stately, but the grounds were unkempt for such a grand place. The winter-brown yard was wild and scraggly. Scattered here and there on high posts were birdhouses.

Maureen led the way when they turned into the yard.

"Maybe she won't be home," Mark said.

"If she doesn't leave home, I'm figuring she'll be in," Maureen said.

They climbed the five steps to the wide porch and stood in front of the tall double front doors. Maureen glanced at Mark.

"You knock," he said.

"If I knock, then you must do the talking," Maureen said. She'd been brave, feeling a kinship with the unknown Mrs. Hoag because they had both suffered bereavement. But standing in front of the imposing doors, she felt small, and again she shivered.

Mark knocked hard on the door, three times. "You can talk. You saw the handbag first."

There was silence inside the house.

Mark knocked again. This time Maureen heard footsteps inside. She held her breath as they waited. From the corner of her eye she saw something move at the side window and knew Mrs. Hoag was looking out to see who was on her large porch. It seemed like an hour before she opened one of the double doors, but it was probably less than a minute.

Maureen wasn't surprised when the door squeaked as the old woman opened it. For a long moment, she stared at Mrs. Hoag. The woman had long dark hair, with barely a hint of gray. It was pulled severely away from her face by large hairpins and hung down her back. Her dark eyes matched her hair. Her eyes were lined with wrinkles as if once long ago she had smiled a lot, but right now her mouth was drawn in a tight line.

"We found your handbag in the creek," Maureen said in a high-pitched voice that she didn't recognize as her own.

"Come inside," Mrs. Hoag said.

Maureen and Mark didn't move.

"Come inside," she repeated and stepped back in her long black mourning dress. "Can't be heating the whole outdoors."

Maureen took a quick breath. Mrs. Hoag was Irish. She sounded just like Maureen's mama when she said that. Maureen quickly walked inside the house and Mark followed.

Mrs. Hoag closed the door, which shut with a creak and a groan; then she led the way through a wide entry hall into a big open room. A fire burned in a large fireplace. Everything in the house was big.

"So you'd be finding my handbag down in the creek," she said. "How do you suspect it got there?"

"We don't know," Maureen said. "It was frozen in the ice by a log when we saw it. When did you lose it?" She moved closer to the fireplace, and Mark followed close behind.

"I didn't lose it. I'm thinking it was stolen."

"We didn't take it," Mark said quickly.

"I didn't say you did, did I?"

Maureen and Mark shook their heads in unison.

Mrs. Hoag opened the clasp and looked inside.

"Some of the things are still frozen," Maureen said.

Mrs. Hoag pulled out the papers and flipped though them. She spotted the money and sat down in a chair to count it.

"Do you know how much is here?" she asked.

"Ninety-six dollars," Mark said.

"Was there a money clip?"

"That's all that was in there. The money was in the compartment under the side flap," Mark explained.

She nodded. "I see. Perhaps the thieves took the money clip and thought that was all the money in here. They must not have searched the bag. I'm finding that strange."

"Yes, it's strange," Maureen said. "Well, we'd best be going." She moved away from the fireplace.

"Wait a moment," Mrs. Hoag said. "What are your names?"

"I'm Maureen O'Callaghan," she said, then quickly added, "Stevenson. This is my cousin, Mark Bowman."

"And where would you be from, Maureen?" Mrs. Hoag asked.

"The Stevensons live about two blocks that way," she said and pointed south.

"I mean in Ireland."

"Castlebar in County Mayo," Maureen answered. There was an interesting glint in Mrs. Hoag's eyes that hadn't been there before that gave Maureen courage to ask, "And you, Mrs. Hoag?"

"Mount Bellew in County Galway. I came over just after the famine. When did you come?"

"Our boat docked at New York on May 14, 1895, nearly eight years ago." It was a day Maureen would never forget.

"Who was with you?"

"My mama and papa," Maureen said with a catch in her throat.

"Where are they now?" Mrs. Hoag asked softly.

"Sleeping with the angels," Maureen whispered.

It was almost as if the old woman willed the words out of Maureen. She told her the little she remembered about her papa, who'd been killed at work in a construction accident shortly after they had arrived in the United States. Maureen and her mama had immediately moved to Minneapolis, where her mama had found work as a live-in cook for Theodore and Nadine Stevenson. Eight months ago they had moved with the Stevensons to their new house near Mrs. Hoag's home. They had been happy there until three months ago, when her mama had caught the flu. She'd thought it was nothing; but the fever had burned her up, and within a week she was dead.

With no family in the United States and none that she knew of in Ireland, Maureen had never felt so alone. She had cried over her mama and cried over her future. And Nadine Stevenson had cried with her and told her that she would be her new mother. She was unable to have children of her own and had always wanted a daughter. She said she'd known Maureen since she was four years old and loved her. She wouldn't think of sending her to an orphanage. The only thing to do was start legal proceedings to adopt Maureen.

In one horrible, long afternoon, Maureen had moved from the downstairs servants' quarters that she'd shared with her mama to an upstairs bedroom down the hall from her new parents. It was too much to take in. A month later, it was official; she was Maureen O'Callaghan Stevenson.

As Maureen wound up her tale, she blinked back tears.

"Nadine Stevenson is a fine woman," Mrs. Hoag said.

"You know her?" Maureen asked.

"Yes. I knew her in the past."

"Before your husband died and you never left your house?" Mark asked. Then he covered his mouth with his hand.

Mrs. Hoag gave him a long hard look. "You're finding it odd that I don't go out and do like I once did?"

"It's just that folks say you're. . ." His voice trailed off.

Maureen couldn't believe that Mark had nearly told Mrs. Hoag that people called her crazy.

"We think it's time you got out again," Maureen said, trying to cover for Mark's blunder. "It doesn't help to stay alone too much." She was normally a quiet girl, but sharing her grief had made her bold, and she continued.

"It helps to talk about losing someone. It helped me just now to tell you about me mama. . .*my* mama," she corrected herself, remembering what her teacher had said about speaking English correctly. "I'm thinking it would help you to talk about your husband and get back to doing whatever were your normal activities before he died."

Now it was Maureen's turn to get that long look from Mrs. Hoag. Had she overstepped her bounds? It was so hard to know these days where the line was. She'd been the cook's daughter. Now she was the banker's daughter. How was she to make sense of so many changes?

"You may be right," Mrs. Hoag said. "I've been giving that some thought lately."

Just then a voice came from behind Maureen and Mark. "Put your hands up! Put your hands up!"

They stuck their hands up over their heads. Had whoever stolen Mrs. Hoag's purse come back to steal again? Maureen glanced at Mark, who was staring straight ahead, his eyes huge. Mrs. Hoag sat in front of them, her face screwed up, cackling a high, crazy laugh.

Who was behind them? And what was wrong with Mrs. Hoag? She was pounding on her knee now. Mark's face had gone white.

"What do you want?" Maureen finally said, lowering her arms.

When she could stop cackling, Mrs. Hoag said, "That was Ruthie."

"Ruthie?" Maureen repeated.

"Put your hands up!" the voice said again.

Maureen stuck her hands back up and slowly turned her head to see who was talking. She looked back at Mrs. Hoag, who started laughing all over again.

"It's a bird," Maureen told Mark.

He turned around, then stuffed his hands in the pockets of his coat.

"Actually, Ruthie's a parrot. Franklin and I brought her back from the West Indies. My husband and I used to travel around the world together. He's the one who taught her to talk."

Ruthie waddled over to her owner.

"Why isn't she in a cage?" Mark asked.

"No need for that. She gets the run of the house since it's only me and Bertha living here."

"She's very good," Maureen said. "Well, we'd best be leaving." The instant kinship she'd felt toward Mrs. Hoag had changed. Seeing her laugh like that made the rumors seem a little more like the truth. Maybe Mrs. Hoag did have a crazy streak.

"Were you expecting a reward for bringing my handbag to me?"

"No," Maureen answered at the same time that Mark said, "Yes."

"You're an honest boy," Mrs. Hoag said. "I'll tell you what. I'll be thinking about it. Come back Monday afternoon around three o'clock, and we'll decide what to do about a reward."

CHAPTER 2

So Many Changes

"Do you think she'll give us money?" Mark asked as they walked to Maureen's house.

"I don't know. Now that we've met her, do you think she's crazy?"

"No. Odd, maybe, but not crazy. Someone who was crazy wouldn't think about giving us a reward."

"Why not?"

"Because that would be normal thinking, and crazy people don't think normal. Wonder what the reward will be."

They turned up the long drive that led to the Stevensons' new house.

"Don't you think her laugh sounded like a maniac's?" Maureen asked.

"No. That parrot was funny," Mark said.

It struck Maureen that she and Mark had switched positions on Mrs. Hoag's sanity now that they had met her. Most of the time they were in agreement on things. Because of that, and because at ten, almost eleven, she was just a year older than Mark and he was the closest to her age of all her new cousins, he had become her best friend. On Saturdays they played together like this, except most days had been less adventurous than this one.

"Uncle Theodore's home," Mark said and pointed to the

automobile that was parked near the detached covered carriage house that had been specially built for it.

That horseless carriage was another new change for Maureen. She'd become accustomed to riding in it now, but only a few months ago she'd never ridden in a contraption like that. It was noisy, but it gave her a grand feeling of elegance.

The house also gave her a regal feeling. It wasn't a huge mansion like Mrs. Hoag's, but it was very large, especially for three people. Actually, there were four now, if she counted the new cook who'd been hired to take her mother's job. Greta lived in Maureen's old room, with the same furniture that Maureen and her mama had used, the same window, and the same door; but now all was different. The blackness of grief settled over Maureen, and she rubbed her forehead with her hand, as if the physical motion could wipe away the pain.

"Better to concentrate on the moment," Nadine Stevenson had told her. "Get through day by day, and each day will get easier." Some days worked like that and moved life forward, and some days worked the opposite way and made Maureen look back too long. Had it been meeting Mrs. Hoag, another Irish woman, that had her thinking of her mama?

The moment. Concentrate on the moment. She turned her attention back to what Mark was saying.

"Do you think Uncle Theodore will let me drive? Father lets me drive the wagon when we get one from the livery." Mark walked around the automobile, admiring the shiny metal.

"I think handling horses and handling an engine are not the same thing," Maureen said. "But I guess it's up to you to be asking him."

She didn't know Theodore Stevenson all that well, but he had always been kind to her. He left for the bank first thing in the morning. Although they shared breakfast and dinner, many nights he went into his study and his wife sometimes went to temperance meetings, leaving Maureen to entertain herself after she'd done her schoolwork. Other nights they'd all sit together, and one of them would read aloud from magazines. Most nights ended with reading one chapter from the Bible.

Maureen knew they worked at being good parents, but they had busy lives that didn't always include a daughter. After the adoption papers had been signed two months ago, the three of them had sat down and discussed their new lives. The Stevensons had assured Maureen that they wouldn't try to take the place of her mama and they welcomed the responsibilities of being new parents.

It was agreed that Maureen would call them *Mother* and *Father*. That was fine with her. She'd called her real parents *Mama* and *Papa*, so it wouldn't be like she was calling the Stevensons by her parents' names.

"I'll get Uncle Theodore to take us both for a ride," Mark said, bringing her back to the present. He and his uncle shared a liking for newfangled things, and Maureen would certainly put the automobile in that category.

They climbed the stairs to the porch and entered the house through the front door, another change that Maureen was getting used to. When they had first moved to the brand-new house eight months ago, she'd entered through the kitchen door in back.

"Uncle Theodore," Mark called and ran into the large front parlor.

"Hey, young fellow, what are you up to?" Maureen's new father stood tall and straight in front of the fireplace. His slender arm rested on the mantel, and he held a cup of coffee in his other hand. "Maureen, how are you this morning?"

"I'm fine, Father," Maureen answered. She wished she could talk to him in the same easy way that Mark did.

"Will you take us for a ride, Uncle Theodore?" Mark asked. "How is she running? How fast have you got her to go?"

"Too fast," Maureen's new mother said as she entered the room. "Mark, you're talking about that automobile as if it were a person. Next thing I know, you'll have named it. Maureen, have you had a pleasant morning?"

"Yes, Mother."

"Let's name her," Mark said. "We could call her something crazy. Like Racing Betty." He glanced at Maureen as if he was sharing a secret. "Or Mrs. Hoag."

"Mrs. Hoag. Our neighbor?" Mother asked.

"Yes. Mark and I were down by that little creek, and we found Mrs. Hoag's handbag and took it to her. She said she knows you."

"Yes. We've met at some community functions, but I don't really know her well. Her husband died a couple years ago, and she's not come out of mourning yet. She rarely leaves her home."

"We know. Maureen told her she should get out more," Mark said.

"Our quiet Maureen?" Mother raised her eyebrows as if surprised that Maureen had said that. Maureen was surprised she'd said it, too, and she wouldn't have if Mark hadn't nearly told Mrs. Hoag what people said about her.

"Mark called her 'Crazy Old Lady Hoag.' Do you think that's true?" Maureen asked.

"I'll let you two talk about that," Father said. "Mark, let's go tinker with the engine a little. It ran a bit rough this morning. We'll call you, Maureen, when we're ready to take her out." Father took big strides to catch up with Mark, who was running toward the door with a big grin on his face.

"Maureen," Mother said when they were the only ones left in the room, "tell me about your visit to Mrs. Hoag."

"She laughed about her parrot scaring us."

"She laughed? From what I've heard, she's not done that in a long while, although she used to be quite a cheerful woman. When her husband was alive, they traveled a great deal. They went around the world a couple times. She spoke once at my women's club meeting about her visit to China." Mother's dark eyes sparkled with curiosity. "I've never been in that mansion. What's it like?"

"Big. I don't know much else. I looked at her the whole time we were there." Maureen explained about the possibility of a reward on Monday. "Is it all right if I go back there? You don't think she's mad, do you, like people say?"

"I think she's still grieving for her husband like you are for your mama. That doesn't make her mad, does it?"

"No." That was something Maureen could understand. "Mark's been guessing what the reward will be."

As if he knew she'd mentioned him, Mark burst into the room.

"We're ready. Are you coming, Aunt Nadine?"

"No, I've got some temperance committee work to do before our next meeting."

Maureen scurried out behind Mark. He climbed in the front seat beside Father, which left the back seat for her.

They took off with a roar down the asphalt street at a sedate five miles an hour; but even at that speed, the wind chilled Maureen, and she pulled her coat tighter.

"Won't she go faster than this?" Mark asked.

Father laughed. "Yes. I've had her up to fifteen, but not today."

They rode along past Mrs. Hoag's mansion. Once the smooth asphalt surface changed to brick, Maureen held onto the seat as the car jostled and the sound of the wheels changed to *click, clack, click, click, clack.*

"Would you teach me to drive?" Mark asked. "My father lets me drive the wagon."

"There's a difference between handling horses and driving an automobile."

"That's what Maureen said, too."

Father turned his head and glanced back at Maureen. "Is that so? Well, we're in agreement. You have to know what makes a car run before you get behind the driving wheel. But I'll be glad to teach you. We'll take it a little each time." He explained the starting crank and brake and gas pedals and showed Mark how turning the driving wheel steered the wheels.

They drove downtown, along the Mississippi River, and then he turned the car back toward home.

"I suspect it'll be a long time before all the streets are paved smooth, but it sure would be nice," Father said.

Maureen agreed. She had been jarred a powerful lot in the backseat.

They were on the brick streets when the front left tire went flat. Father dug the toolbox out of the boot, and Maureen watched as he taught Mark how to patch the tube. Within half an hour they were back on the road.

"You have to be prepared for things like that," Father said.

"Like when a horse throws a shoe," Mark said.

They detoured by Mark's house and dropped him off, and Maureen climbed into the front seat. Near home, as they passed Mrs. Hoag's house, Father shouted over the roar of the motor, "I don't think she's crazy."

Maureen nodded.

Once they were in the driveway, Father shut off the engine but didn't make a move to get out of the automobile, so Maureen sat still.

"Mrs. Hoag's account is at our bank. She has her housekeeper come in and make withdrawals for her whenever she needs money. That may be odd, but Mrs. Hoag knows so many people, and if she were out in public, she'd run into people she knows. She may not have the courage to face them yet. She may be afraid someone will mention her husband and she'll get emotional. You'd think in two years' time, the pain would have healed some. But it's different for everyone." He cleared his throat and continued. "She might have done better if she'd had someone to talk to about him. I want you to know that you can always talk to me about your mama or papa. I want to be a good father to you."

"Thank you," Maureen said.

Father opened his door, signaling an end to what Maureen considered an uncomfortable conversation.

She wanted desperately to love the Stevensons. And she did love them in her own way. She'd known them for seven years, but as the kind employers of her mama, not as her parents.

That evening, as if they were making a new effort to reach her, the

Stevensons sat in the parlor with Maureen. Mother read aloud from *Life on the Mississippi* by Mark Twain.

"I wonder if he was ever up this far north on the Mississippi," Father mused.

"I've read that he's given a lecture tour in Europe. If he comes to Minneapolis, we should go hear him," Mother said. "He's supposed to be quite entertaining." She read a few chapters, then picked up the Bible and flipped to the place where they'd left off the night before. She read a chapter, and they discussed it before they went upstairs to their bedrooms.

Maureen climbed into her bed and stared up at the lovely pink canopy above her. She felt like a princess in this bed and in this room. The pink rose wallpaper was elegant. She even had her own bathroom. This was living a high life that she'd never dreamed of, but she would trade it all away and be quite happy downstairs in the servants' quarters if only her mama were alive.

She wiped her eyes as a quiet knock sounded on her door a moment before her new mother opened it.

"Ready?"

"Yes, Mother."

As was her custom each night, Mother knelt at the side of the bed with Maureen and they said a prayer. It always started out the same, "Dear Lord, thank You for this day. And please let us have cheerful moments tomorrow."

Maureen knew that sentence was for her. It fit in with Mother's day-by-day, concentrate-on-the-moment way of getting through grief. Five years ago, Mother's father had died; and three years ago, her mother had died. She'd confided in Maureen that she still had days when she cried about them. She understood the pain that sat like a weight on Maureen's heart, and somehow that helped.

They finished the prayer, and Mother kissed Maureen on the cheek.

"Good night, my daughter," she said.

"Good night, Mother," Maureen said.

The next morning the family went to church together, which had been another change for Maureen. The church she had attended with her mama was steeped in ritual. The burning incense, the lighted candles, and the Latin words that the parishioners recited by heart were what Maureen associated with church. The Stevensons' church lacked these traditions. Other children her age were in her new Sunday school class, which met before she sat in the hard wooden pew with her new parents for the church service. When a member of the congregation had shouted out "Amen" at the end of the parson's prayer the first time Maureen had attended the church, she had been horrified.

"We all worship the same God," Mother had told her after that service. "We just do it in different ways. The important thing is to love the Lord and accept Him as your Savior."

The asking for saving part was a new concept to Maureen; but after it was explained to her, she believed it and was baptized into the Stevensons' church just a month after she'd been adopted. This Sunday she stood in the hallway that led to the sanctuary, waiting for Mother and Father to come out of their Sunday school class.

"Good morning, Maureen," Mark's mother said as she walked toward her.

"Good morning, Aunt Annie," Maureen said. She had liked

Mark's mother from the moment she had met her. She was plump—
full-figured, Maureen's mama had called her—and she loved everyone. It showed in her smile and in her eyes.

"I understand you and Mark are going to see Mrs. Hoag
tomorrow after school. That should be most interesting."

"Do you know her?" Maureen asked.

"I met her once. She's quite a traveler. A few years ago, she was
always in the middle of whatever was happening in Minneapolis.
But since her husband died, her personality has changed. She's the
opposite of the woman she used to be."

The opposite, Maureen thought. Was that another way of saying
she was crazy?

CHAPTER 3

Spreading Rumors

Monday morning Maureen walked to school, dragging her feet. She didn't fit in with the others. The change hadn't come when the Stevensons had moved to the brand new house on Mrs. Hoag's street, because Maureen had continued to go to the same public school as when she and her mama had lived with the Stevensons in their old house.

But as Maureen O'Callaghan, she'd been friends with the group of girls who were daughters of other servants. Now that she was Maureen Stevenson, her former friends treated her as if they thought she was too good for them.

It had been a gradual change. At first the girls had felt sorry for her because her mama had died. But when Maureen's wardrobe changed from altered secondhand clothing to new store-bought dresses, their attitudes toward her changed as well.

She was pushed out of one social group, but the wealthier girls wouldn't accept her into their circle, either. They teased her about her Irish brogue, which was the same as telling her she didn't belong.

Maureen just wanted to fit in. She needed friends, and again she latched on to Mark Bowman, even though he was a year behind her in school. At outdoor playtimes, she talked to him since no one else included her. Several times she noticed odd looks from other boys Mark's age. She knew she should leave him alone so he could play with them, but she needed someone. And he seemed willing to be with her—especially today.

"Mother said I could walk home with you so we could go straight to Crazy Old Lady Hoag's," he said when the students were outside playing after eating their noon meal. Maureen and Mark stood in the bright sunlight on the side of the school building that blocked the wind. Other children milled close by. One girl stopped and stared at them.

"You're going to Crazy Old Lady Hoag's?" Sarah Noble asked with disbelief in her voice. She was in Maureen's grade, and she was from one of the wealthier families in Minneapolis.

"We're going there after school," Maureen said. "What do you know about Mrs. Hoag?"

Some of Sarah's other friends gathered around them.

"They say she's quite mad," Sarah said. "She never comes out of her house except to feed birds. They call her the bird woman."

"She only has one servant in that mansion," another girl said. "She does everything for Crazy Old Lady Hoag, who sits and stares out the window. She doesn't talk to anybody."

"She talks to her parrot," Maureen said. "And the bird talks back!"

"What does it say?" Sarah asked.

Maureen glanced at Mark and hoped he wouldn't give away how scared they had been when Ruthie had told them to put up their hands and they had thought a burglar had been in the house.

"Mrs. Hoag's husband taught it to talk, so it says all sorts of things."

"Naughty things? Like a pirate's parrot would say?" Sarah asked.

Maureen nodded, even though she hadn't heard Ruthie say anything except "Put your hands up."

"They say Mrs. Hoag belongs in an insane asylum," Sarah informed them. "They say she's gone crazy since her husband died."

"She must have loved him very much," Maureen said. "And who is *they* who says all this?" Although she'd given Sarah and her friends more information to add to the rumor mill, she felt disloyal to Mrs. Hoag and wished she could take back the remark about the parrot. She'd so wanted to fit in with the girls that she'd stretched the truth.

"*They* is everybody," Sarah said. "People all over town know about her."

Mark had been quiet, but now he jumped in to defend the old lady. "She's giving us a reward for finding her stolen handbag. Somebody who should be in an insane asylum doesn't give rewards."

"What kind of reward?" Sarah asked. "And what was in her handbag?"

"We'll find out the reward this afternoon," Maureen said. "It's cold out here. I'm going inside." She wasn't going to stand around and add more wood to the fire of public opinion against Mrs. Hoag. "Coming, Mark?"

As they turned to walk inside, she heard Sarah telling yet another girl about Mrs. Hoag. What had Maureen started by her careless remark about that parrot?

"I'm sorry I said anything to her," she told Mark. Telling tales wasn't a Christian thing to do, and in her mind she asked God's forgiveness, just as Mother had taught her to do.

"Why did you say it?" he asked. "She really thinks Mrs. Hoag is crazy. So do the others."

"I know," Maureen said without explaining her reasons for exaggerating the story about Ruthie. "I'm sorry," she said again as she went into her classroom.

The night before, Mother had told Maureen that she'd be coming to school for the WCTU, and during the afternoon session, Maureen's teacher called the class to attention.

"In addition to our regular study of the evil of alcohol, we're pleased to have a representative from the Women's Christian Temperance Union. Each of the other classrooms has a WCTU member visiting today to help with a demonstration. Mrs. Stevenson is in our room because of her daughter. Maureen, would you like to introduce our guest to the class?"

Maureen felt her face flush. She hadn't known she'd have to speak in front of the whole class, but she couldn't disobey her teacher. She slowly stood and walked to the front of the room where Mother waited.

"My mother, Mrs. Stevenson, is vice president of the Minneapolis chapter of the Women's Christian Temperance Union. She works very hard for the group and wants to stop alcohol from taking over the lives of many people." She'd heard her mother say that often enough.

Maureen quickly walked back to her seat. Why couldn't Mother be more like Mark's mother? Aunt Annie stayed at home and took care of her family. She didn't go into the schools or carry signs outside places that served alcohol. Mother had even been arrested once for demonstrating at a saloon, but she didn't stay in jail more than an hour before she was out. Father had made sure of that.

Mother had laughed it off and said it was part of the plan.

Arrests gave reporters something to write about, and the more people knew about the movement, the stronger the temperance movement became.

"Thank you, Maureen," Mother said. "Today, members of the WCTU have come to your school to demonstrate what alcohol can do to your brain." She pulled a clear glass jar from the large canvas bag she had set on the floor.

"This is part of a cow's brain. Notice how pink it is? That's because this cow was healthy and never drank hard liquor."

Maureen glanced around as the students tittered over a cow drinking alcohol. Mother had the attention of her classmates. Maureen nervously wrung her hands in her lap as she focused on the attractive woman at the front of the room.

"Now, in this bottle is alcohol." Mother uncorked the bottle and poured it onto the cow's brain. The pink color changed to a nasty gray.

The entire class gasped, Maureen along with them. Oohs and ahs filled the air.

"This could happen to your brain if you drink alcoholic brews. If you know someone who drinks liquor or if your parents keep alcohol in your house, why not try this simple demonstration to show them what harm it is doing to them?"

The class applauded and Maureen took a deep breath. She couldn't analyze the feeling she'd had while her mother was speaking, but she'd been nervous.

"Next week, I'll come again, and we'll practice the poem 'Counting Fingers.' I've brought copies for each of you so that you can be memorizing it. Some of you may already know it from your Sunday school. Maureen, would you pass these out?"

Maureen made her way to the front of the room again, took the papers, and distributed them to her classmates while Mother packed up her jar and bottle.

"Thank you, dear. And thank you, boys and girls, for being good listeners."

Again the class applauded as she left the room. The teacher began the history lesson, and Maureen let her mind wander to what would happen later that afternoon.

As soon as school was over, Maureen met Mark by the flag-pole, and they walked toward Mrs. Hoag's mansion.

"You can't slip up and call her 'Crazy Old Lady Hoag' like you almost did last time," Maureen said. She made him say "Mrs. Hoag" over and over until it was second nature to him, and she said it under her breath so that it was natural to her, too.

"Do you think she'll give us money?" Mark asked.

"I don't know," Maureen said. "What would you do if she did?"

"I'd get parts to fix Calvin's bicycle. When he left for college he said I could have it, but it's got a bent shaft and needs a new front wheel. You could ride my sister Eva's bicycle, and we could go all over town."

They quickened their pace as they neared Mrs. Hoag's grounds. Thick clouds had moved in and covered the sun, giving the impression that it would snow. The dismal-looking gray day made the mansion look sinister.

Was there anything to the rumors that Mrs. Hoag was crazy? Maureen shook her head to dislodge that thought from settling there.

They climbed the front steps, and again Mark did the knock-ing. Mrs. Hoag immediately opened the door, as if she had been standing on the other side. She wore a maroon dress, a startling change from the black mourning dress she'd worn on Saturday. The color gave her a younger appearance and seemed to put a sparkle in her old eyes.

"Come in," she invited, and they stepped into the entry hall.

They followed Mrs. Hoag into the same room that they had been in before. This time Maureen looked around so she could tell her new mother and Aunt Annie about it. An oriental rug covered the space between the couch and the fireplace. The curtains were dark green and heavy looking. Double doors led out to a side porch. Vases covered with dragons sat on several small tables. There were dozens of the urn-shaped vessels.

Mrs. Hoag told them to sit on the couch facing the fireplace. A low table held little cookies, teacups, and a fancy silver teapot. Mrs. Hoag poured them each a cup of hot tea.

Maureen took hers with milk to cool it, while Mark doctored his with sugar.

"These cookies are very good," Maureen said politely.

"Why, thank you," Mrs. Hoag answered.

After they'd each had two cookies and Mrs. Hoag had refilled their teacups, Mark asked the question. "Have you thought any more about the reward?"

"I see you like to get directly to the point," Mrs. Hoag answered. "I have given considerable thought to the reward, as well as to other matters. I do believe your honesty should be rewarded. That is the most important trait a person can have. Mark, your parents have taught you well. Maureen, the values your mama and Nadine Stevenson have instilled in you will allow you to take your proper place in life, although right now you may be thinking you don't know where that may be."

Maureen wondered if Mrs. Hoag was a mind reader. Where was Maureen's rightful place in life?

"I remember when I first came to this country. It was 1851. That was over fifty years ago. I was but a girl of seventeen, on my own, trying to make my way in a strange land. I remember as if it were yesterday the ship docking and the hope and fear on the faces of the other passengers. We thought this was the land of milk and honey. And for some of us, it was. Within my first year here, I met Franklin Hoag and married him. I didn't know at the time that he was from a wealthy family. I met him in New York, when he was returning from a grand tour of Europe. We knew each other three days before we married."

She took another drink of tea and stared into space.

"It was in this very room that he introduced me to his parents as his wife. You haven't seen such a to-do over nothing. You'd have thought he'd done something terribly wrong—marrying an Irish lass." She chuckled. "His mother finally came to accept me, but not before she tried her best to make me over."

She laughed again. "She wasn't very successful. She said I had too much of my own mind, but she taught me the proper way of society. She said that with wealth came responsibility to help others and do good things. She was a very Christian woman, and I think she respected me in spite of my background. Once she told me that if her only son loved me, then she would love me, too."

Maureen glanced at Mark, who was shifting on the couch. He leaned too far forward and spilt some tea on his trousers.

Mrs. Hoag handed him a linen napkin to soak it up. "Getting fidgety, are you? Then I'll get to the reward and save my life story for another time. Knowing how important money is to your generation, and since I have recovered my ninety-six dollars, I've decided to give you each ten dollars."

"Ten dollars!" Maureen said.

"Wow!" Mark exclaimed. "I can fix my brother's bike."

Mrs. Hoag got out her handbag, a different one than the one they had fished out of the creek. She made quite a ceremony of taking out two crisp ten-dollar bills. When she handed one to each of them, they said thank you. Then they stared at each other. Maureen thought it was time to go, but Mrs. Hoag wasn't through talking.

"As I said, I've also given some thought to some other things." She paused for a moment, as if wondering how to phrase what she wanted to say.

"Before you came on Saturday, I'd been thinking that I had settled into a bad routine. I've been living with memories instead of making new ones. Your unexpected visit was what I needed to see that life goes on. Maureen, you've suffered the loss of your mama lately, but you've not let it get you down."

Maureen would have argued that point. Some days she did fine, and other days were horrible, with a darkness settling over her that wouldn't leave.

"I'm ready to move forward now, too," Mrs. Hoag continued. "And I'd like to hire you two to work for me."

"You want us to work for you?" Maureen asked in astonishment. Mrs. Hoag must be ready to hire a full housekeeping staff. "Doing what?" She had helped her mama in the kitchen doing dishes and various chores, but she didn't know if her new mother would want her to work as a servant again.

"As I said earlier, with wealth comes responsibility. My husband and I traveled a great deal when he was alive. We collected many souvenirs and artworks from abroad, and we decorated each room with items from a specific country or region. This is our Oriental Room."

Maureen had already figured that out from all the dragon vases.

"As I get older, the house seems bigger than ever. I misplace things, and I'm getting forgetful. Yesterday I was sure I'd put some bookends in here on that table. But the next time I saw them, they were in the kitchen, and Bertha said she hadn't moved them. Sometimes I get frightened living here. I hear odd noises and voices at night, but I hate to leave. This was my husband's family home," she said quietly. Her voice got stronger as she got back to the subject of the job.

"We could start on the top floor and go room by room, cataloging the contents. I can't remember where several items are, and I need an inventory of my belongings for insurance purposes. I need help doing that. Bertha has her hands full keeping this house up, so I need to hire extras to assist me. Some of the items are quite valuable, and I know I can trust you two because of your honesty in bringing that handbag to me."

"What do you pay?" Mark asked.

"I thought I'd start with ten cents an hour and see how that goes and what kind of workers you are. I believe industry should be encouraged."

"Get down. Put your hands up!" Maureen knew it was Ruthie before she turned her head and saw the parrot waddle into the room. She wasn't going to be fooled twice by that bird.

"Hey, Ruthie, what you doing?" Mark baby-talked to the bird.

Mrs. Hoag ignored Ruthie and got back to business. "What do you think of my job offer?"

"I'll do it," Mark said immediately.

"We must ask our mothers," Maureen said. She couldn't commit to this without permission from the Stevensons, nor did she think Mark should without his parents' consent. "Could we call you?"

"That would be fine. I'd like you to work on Tuesdays and Thursdays after school and on Saturdays. When school is out for the summer, we can plan on more days."

"I'll call you this evening," Maureen said.

CHAPTER 4

The Job

"Did she say she heard voices?" Maureen asked Mark as they walked down Mrs. Hoag's drive. That sounded like a crazy person. She'd heard of lunatics obeying the voices they heard in their heads and going out and harming people.

"She said she heard noises in the night. The voices could be people passing on the street," Mark said.

"Maybe." Maureen wasn't convinced. That Irish kinship she felt for Mrs. Hoag argued with her common sense. Mrs. Hoag had been an entirely different person than the one they had met on Saturday. Oh, she'd explained that she'd mourned long enough and it was time to get on with life, but could a person really change her ways that fast?

"What will Aunt Nadine say about the job offer?" Mark asked.

"I don't know. Do you want to do it?"

"Yes. We'll have our own spending money, and I'll get out of chores at home," Mark said and laughed.

Maureen considered the idea of having money of her own. In the old days, as she now referred to the time when her mama was alive, she'd sometimes earned a dime or two that she could spend as she liked at the candy shop or the soda fountain. Now the Stevensons gave her everything she needed. So far she hadn't asked to go anywhere with the girls after school, but she had hoped to go roller skating soon. In the old days, she'd been allowed to skate on an occasional Saturday afternoon. Maybe her old friends would skate with her then.

Yes, the idea of having money of her own and not having to ask Mother and Father for it was most appealing.

They arrived at the end of Mrs. Hoag's short drive and parted, Mark going north toward his home and Maureen turning south to walk the two blocks to the Stevenson house.

"Mother?" Maureen called when she walked into the front hall. There was no answer. She put her schoolbook on the hall table and peeked into the parlor. "Mother?" But the room was empty. She followed the smell of baking apple pies and walked toward the back of the house. "Mother?"

"Mrs. Stevenson's at a meeting," Greta answered from the kitchen. "Some days I think she'll get rid of alcohol in this city single-handedly."

"She talked about it at school today," Maureen said. She picked up the dish towel and began drying dishes, as she had in the old days when she'd come home to find her mama preparing the evening meal.

"You better get on out of here. Wouldn't do for Mrs. Stevenson to see you doing my work. She wants to raise you to take your proper place in the world, and that shouldn't be in a kitchen. You should grow up to be a fine lady like her."

"Why did they adopt me?" Maureen had wanted to know Greta's opinion for some time but had never had the opportunity to ask. Servants usually knew everything that was going on.

Greta tilted her head in thought, then said, "Because they're good Christian people, and they knew you needed them as much as they needed you. They must have thought God had sent you to be their daughter."

"Do you mean they think God had Mama die just so they could adopt me?"

"No, just that there's a purpose to things and all things work out." Greta shook her head, which made her large body shake, too. "You're too smart for your own good." Greta grabbed the dish towel from her. "Now, scat, missy."

Maureen wandered back into the hall, then carried her book upstairs to her room. She had arithmetic homework to do, but she made no attempt to start it. Instead, she plopped on her bed and looked up at the lacy pink canopy.

So, she was to become a lady and take her rightful place in the world.

"Where would that be, Mama?" she said aloud. She remembered stories Mama had told of the old country and how poor they'd been there before coming to America to seek their fortune. It was much as Mrs. Hoag had described it. The land of milk and honey. "Is this what you want for me, Mama?" Maureen asked the canopy.

She couldn't remember the old country. She'd been almost three when her family had immigrated. She didn't remember the trip over or their time in New York—just the day they had docked at Ellis Island was etched in her memory. All she had were mental pictures of Papa, as her mother had described him.

Maureen wanted to talk to Mrs. Hoag again. She wanted to learn about Ireland, and she wanted to know more about her own past.

Maureen pushed off the bed and crossed the large room to her dresser. She picked up the wooden picture frame and stared at her mama and herself on the back porch. Her new father had taken the picture on the day they had all moved to the new house. It had been a joyous day. Mama's wide smile had shown how pleased she was to have a brand new kitchen and the most modern stove the Stevensons could buy from the Sears catalog.

"Maureen, dear," Mother's voice called upstairs, "I'm home."

Maureen gently put the frame down and walked downstairs. Mother hugged her.

"How was the meeting with Mrs. Hoag?" she asked.

Maureen had nearly forgotten about the reward in the excitement about the job. She explained about the tea party, the Oriental Room, the ten dollars, and the cataloging.

"Mark really wants to do it. May I work for her, too?" she asked, doubting that the job would be what taking her place as a lady in the world meant.

"Let's decide over dinner." Maureen interpreted her mother's remark to mean that she wanted Father's opinion.

Mark called shortly before dinner to say that he'd gotten permission to work for Mrs. Hoag. That would be one more argument for taking the job.

After Father arrived home from the bank and the family was seated at the dinner table, he asked the Lord's blessing on the food. Maureen added a silent prayer for Father's approval of the job.

As soon as Greta had served the roast and potatoes, Maureen repeated her story about the visit with Mrs. Hoag.

"You're to call her tonight?" Father asked.

"Yes. I'd like to take the job," Maureen said.

"She'd learn about other cultures and their art," he said to Mother. "And Mrs. Hoag could use a push to get back into life. I think it's a good idea, but I'd like to go over and talk to Mrs. Hoag instead of just letting Maureen call her."

Maureen looked at Mother expectantly.

"Then it's settled, but I think we should all go over together. I'd like a peek at that house," she said with a playful smile and a gleam in her eyes.

As soon as the meal was over, Maureen called Mark and told him the good news. She telephoned Mrs. Hoag as she'd promised and asked if they could call on her. Then the small Stevenson family climbed into the automobile and drove the two blocks to Mrs. Hoag's home.

"We could have walked," Mother shouted above the roar as they turned into Mrs. Hoag's drive.

"I know," Father said, "but I wanted to try the lights out. I haven't used them much."

Ahead of them the dim headlights illuminated another automobile parked near the front door.

"Sidney Orr is here," Father said. "I didn't know he knew Mrs. Hoag."

"How do you know it's him?" Mother asked.

"That's his automobile. It's the only one like it in town." Father jumped down from the driver's side and opened the doors for Mother and Maureen. Then he hurried ahead to admire the automobile.

Maureen could barely make out the other automobile, so she knew Father couldn't see much either, but he was stroking it as if it were a favorite horse.

"Fine automobile," he said and reluctantly left it to walk with them to the front door.

Father knocked, and a long moment passed before the door was opened.

"Hello, Mrs. Hoag. We're sorry to interrupt your evening," he said, "but we wanted to talk to you about Maureen's new job."

"And to bring you a freshly baked apple pie," Mother said. She held the pie out, and Mrs. Hoag took it and set it on a parson's bench in the hallway.

"Come in," she said brusquely. She still wore the maroon dress, which looked festive, but her expression was not as warm as it had been that afternoon. "Let me take your wraps."

As soon as their coats were hung on the hall tree, she led the way to the Oriental Room. A man sitting on the couch rose when they walked in. He was rather stocky, and his head was balding in front. He smiled a friendly greeting.

"Hello, Sidney," Father said. "A pleasure to see you again."

"Good evening, Theodore," Sidney Orr said. "I didn't know you knew my dear friend."

"We're new neighbors," Father said. "Fine automobile you have. German-made, isn't it?"

"Please sit down," Mrs. Hoag said. "I see you know Sidney, who surprised me with this visit. His father and my husband were lifelong friends."

"Ah," Father said, as if understanding the connection. He introduced Sidney to Mother and Maureen and explained that Sidney was a lawyer and occasionally had dealings with the bank. As soon as the ladies were seated, the men sat down.

"We've meant to come before now," Mother said. "We'd like

to be good neighbors."

Mrs. Hoag offered a tight smile. "How nice," she said, although the words came out without expression. The change in her surprised Maureen, who studied Mrs. Hoag's face, looking for a reason for her dourness.

"Sidney, you were saying?" Mrs. Hoag prompted her old friend in a cold voice.

He glanced hesitantly at Father, then spoke. "I was merely reminding you that we had talked at some length about your selling the land to me. You told me the house was much too large for you and Bertha to keep up, and you were considering moving to a smaller place. You said you'd let me be the first to know when you had decided."

"I don't recall the conversation," she said, "but I haven't decided to sell this place. If I do, I'll let you know. And I won't forget the conversation this time because Maureen will remind me. Right, Maureen? You have a young mind, so you can't be forgetful yet. The years rob us of our memories." She shook her head.

"I'll remember," Maureen assured her, but she hoped Mrs. Hoag wouldn't sell. That would do away with her new job.

Silence descended over the group, and Maureen wondered if she should bring up the reason for their visit, but Father looked at her and gave a brief shake of his head, so she remained quiet. Maybe he wanted to assess Mrs. Hoag's stern behavior before he brought up the subject of the cataloging job.

"Well, I guess I'll be going," Sidney Orr said finally. "It's been a pleasure to see you again, Lillian." He stood up, and Father stood up, too.

Mrs. Hoag remained seated. "I'll see myself out," Mr. Orr said, but Father walked out with him.

"Father likes automobiles," Maureen said to make conversation. "I imagine they are talking about them."

"I'm thinking I'd like one," Mrs. Hoag said as if she'd just that moment decided to get one. "Bertha takes the trolley to run our errands, but I may want to get out myself and not be tied to the trolley schedule. Perhaps Mr. Stevenson can advise me about a horseless carriage."

"I'm sure he'd be pleased to," Mother said. "Mrs. Hoag, we came about the job you've offered Maureen. Are you quite sure you'd like to hire her?"

"I wouldn't be offering if I wasn't wanting her to help me," Mrs. Hoag said with a heavier than usual Irish brogue in her voice.

"You certainly have some fine things," Mother said. "I can see why you'd want to catalog them. These vases are very old, aren't they?"

"Some from the Ming dynasty," Mrs. Hoag said. "But I see where your mind is going, and yours, too, Maureen. Would I like youngsters to be handling them? Might they get broken?"

Mother nodded. "Yes, I wondered about that."

Maureen looked hard at Mrs. Hoag. Was she really a mind reader? That was twice today that she'd known what Maureen had been thinking.

"I have a general insurance policy on my fine things, although there's not a complete listing. That's one reason I want to catalog these items. And what good are things if you can't touch them now and again? I'll be moving most of the items, so there's no need to be fearing what may not happen."

Father knocked on the outside door, then let himself in. He walked quickly into the Oriental Room and sat down again.

"That's a fine automobile Sidney has," he said.

"Where can I get one?" Mrs. Hoag asked.

Father looked taken aback. "One like his? It's German-made, and it's a very fast automobile."

"Not especially like his. Is there a kind I could be handling easier?"

"For around town and for a woman, I'd suggest an electric. I have a Woods catalog, if you'd like me to look into it for you."

"Would you be so kind? I'd like one immediately."

"It takes a while to order one, and then it would have to be shipped by rail. Probably take a month or two, maybe more, but I'll see what I can find out."

"Thank you, Mr. Stevenson. Now the other matter at hand was Maureen's job. I'm sure she'll be excellent help for me. The work will be fitting for a girl her age."

"I'm sure it will be," he said. "Thank you for trusting—"

"Put your hands up," Ruthie said from the hallway, stopping Father in midsentence. "Put your hands up."

He didn't stick his hands up, but he looked stunned.

"It's a parrot," Maureen said.

Mrs. Hoag chuckled, but she didn't laugh that maniacal laugh that she had when Maureen and Mark had thrust their hands in the air.

"My husband said Ruthie was better than a watchdog," she explained. "Thieves would give themselves up if they heard her."

Maureen glanced at Ruthie. Had the parrot seen the burglars who had taken Mrs. Hoag's handbag from the house? And if they were truly thieves, why hadn't they taken the expensive oriental vases? That didn't make sense.

What if nobody took Mrs. Hoag's handbag at all? What if she threw it into the creek herself? But only a crazy person would do that!

CHAPTER 5

Counting Fingers

By noon on Tuesday, everyone in school knew that Maureen and Mark were going to help Mrs. Hoag catalog her artwork. Although Maureen had told no one, Mark had mentioned it to a couple boys, and the news spread like wildfire.

Maureen hadn't anticipated the reaction of her classmates. The daughters of servants were glad that she was going to be working, even if it wasn't a regular chore-type job. The wealthy girls thought she showed great courage in facing Mrs. Hoag. Outside on the playground after the noon meal, Sarah said that Maureen was either brave or stupid, she couldn't decide which, but the other girls shushed her, and Maureen brushed it off as envy from Sarah since Maureen was the center of attention for the day.

Being friends with everyone was what Maureen wanted, but she wondered if the attraction would last. At least tomorrow the others would want to know how the first day working at Mrs. Hoag's had gone.

After school, Maureen and Mark walked quickly to the mansion, although Maureen was tempted to stroll along. It was one of those rare March days when the sun was shining brightly and the temperature said spring was in the air.

"What do you think we'll work on today?" Mark asked as they

climbed the porch steps.

"We'll know soon enough," Maureen said.

"Good afternoon, children," Mrs. Hoag said. She'd opened the door before they could knock. "I've been waiting for you. I'm so anxious to get started."

Maureen hung her coat on the hall tree as she had the night before, and Mark did the same.

"We'll start at the top," Mrs. Hoag said and led the way upstairs. She had piled her hair up on top of her head in a bun. The dress she wore was a dark shade of purple—not as bright as yesterday's maroon dress, but it wasn't a black mourning dress, either.

Maureen and Mark followed her up the wide, wooden staircase that opened onto a large hallway on the second floor. Mrs. Hoag opened a set of double doors, revealing another stairwell. This wasn't as broad as the main staircase, but still Maureen and Mark could climb side by side.

Mrs. Hoag opened the door at the third-floor landing and led the way into a giant room. "This was the ballroom. It's the largest room in the house."

It was huge. Two walls were lined with paintings. Cowboys, Indians, herds of cattle, horses and riders, anything Western hung on those walls. On the dance floor stood at least twenty tables that held statues of more horses and cowboys and Indians.

Ruthie waddled in. "Quiet. Be quiet. Put your hands up!" she said as she walked around the room.

The other two walls were solid windows with a pair of double doors on the front side that led to the balcony. Maureen looked out toward the backyard and saw lots of bird feeders on poles. There had been a few in the front yard, but there must have been fifteen in the back. Birds were eating out of them. A whole flock had landed out there.

Maureen knocked hard on the window, and the sudden noise made the birds lift off in a giant wave. They flew toward the wooded area behind the house.

At this height, Maureen could see the creek. It curved from where they had found the purse to cut right toward Mrs. Hoag's house, then it turned back about a hundred yards away. Maureen hadn't realized it was that close.

"Let's begin," Mrs. Hoag said. "Franklin was fascinated by the West. We went out there several times to different parts. My favorite was the trip in 1885—September, it was—and we stayed three days at Elkhorn Ranch in the Dakota Badlands country. I sat in a rocking chair on the front porch of the ranch house and looked over the Little Missouri River while Franklin went hunting with our host. Guess whose front porch that was?" She had a mischievous look in her eye.

"Whose?" Mark asked.

"President Theodore Roosevelt's," she said proudly. "Oh, he wasn't president then, but he and Franklin were great friends. He wrote me a card after Franklin died. I still have it around somewhere. I kept all the cards people sent to me." That sad, haunted look, the one Maureen had seen the first time she'd met Mrs. Hoag, returned; then Mrs. Hoag shook her head and lifted her chin. "These artworks portray the West as Franklin saw it."

"You saw Indians?" Mark asked.

"Yes, but the ones I saw were peaceful enough," she said. "Not like in some of the artwork." She pointed toward the first wall of pictures. "Let's see how we'll manage this."

While Mrs. Hoag pondered the situation, Maureen wondered about the truth in her statement that she knew President Roosevelt. Was this another claim of a crazy person?

"We must describe each painting," Mrs. Hoag said. "Move that chair over here for me, Mark, and we'll start. You two can call off the name and the artist and give a description of the painting. I'll write it down. Maureen, would you dust each frame as we finish with it?"

The dust cloth, a pen, and paper were on the chair that Mark moved closer to the wall for Mrs. Hoag. Obviously she had been preparing for their work session. A fire blazed in a large fireplace, and the steam heaters clanged and clattered as if they had been recently turned on.

They started on the south wall and worked their way around the room. Maureen admired each painting, and Mrs. Hoag wrote down approximately when she and her husband had purchased it and where, to the best of her memory.

"I should have done this as we added each piece," she said. "Now this one is a favorite of mine. It was the last one we purchased before Franklin died. *The Old Stagecoach of the Plains.* It's a night scene and reminds me of how we traveled once long ago. See the light inside the coach? Remington is a master at capturing a moment of action."

Maureen studied the painting as she dusted its frame. A guard sat on the top of the stage, as if anticipating danger. There was something lonely about the painting and something of adventure in it, too.

"He's very good," she commented.

"If you like this, you'll love his bronzes," Mrs. Hoag said.

"Look over yonder." She pointed to one of the statues in the center of the room. "See how he has the horse rearing?"

Maureen and Mark walked over to the statue.

"That horse is standing on his back legs," Mark said. "How does he balance like that?"

"Frederic Remington told me that he took pictures and then tried to duplicate them. See the roughness of the horse's mane? See his ribs? Look at that one over there." She pointed to a different statue. "*The Wicked Pony.* He's bucking and has thrown his rider. Franklin was thrown once and broke his arm. But he said he didn't regret it. Franklin lived life to its fullest, a lesson we should learn from him."

Before Mrs. Hoag could get maudlin again, Maureen changed the subject. "Do you know Mr. Remington?"

"Oh yes, dear. He and Franklin were good friends. Whenever we were in the East, we'd visit his studio. It took him a while to warm to me, since I was an immigrant, but we've become fairly good friends. I should look into what he's been doing and perhaps get another of his bronzes for our collection. I'll make a note of it, since my memory isn't what it should be."

She jotted something on the edge of the paper, and then they got back to work. They finished the paintings and half the statues before Mrs. Hoag said it was time to quit for the day.

"But you will be back on Thursday?" she asked. "You like this work?"

"Oh yes," Mark said. "Do we keep a record of our hours or do we get paid each day?"

"I can be depending on you to keep sight of the important things," Mrs. Hoag said with a laugh. "I'll pay each Saturday after we finish for the day. Agreed?"

Mark nodded. "If we work Saturday morning, then we can still go skating on Saturday afternoon."

Mrs. Hoag smiled. "That's fine with me."

Maureen and Mark left her at the front door, then they separated at the end of the driveway.

At home, Mother reminded Maureen that she was to accompany her to the WCTU meeting that evening. It was important to Mother, and it was drudgery to Maureen.

She slipped upstairs before dinner to go over the piece Mother wanted her to recite. "Counting Fingers" was the poem her class at school was memorizing for next week, but Maureen had already learned it just for this special meeting.

Mother was involved in getting the evils of alcohol out of the United States, and Maureen respected her for that, but she didn't like getting dragged into the fight. Standing in front of a group and talking bothered her so much. She'd had to do it yesterday at school, and again tonight she'd be on display as Nadine Stevenson's new daughter.

At dinner, Maureen explained about the job. She mentioned the wonderful statues of the horses standing on two legs, but she didn't mention that Mrs. Hoag had said she knew both the artist and the president. Although she harbored thoughts that Mrs. Hoag was exaggerating, she kept quiet out of loyalty to her new employer.

"I'll call on Mrs. Hoag this evening," Father said. "I have the Woods catalog, so she can look at the electrics, but I mentioned at the bank that I was looking into automobiles for her, and Mark's father said he knew of one here in town for sale. The estate of Mr.

Thomas Swain is being settled, and he had just acquired a Road-Wagon before he died. I think it would be perfect for Mrs. Hoag, and she could get it now instead of waiting a few months."

The telephone rang, two longs and a short, the Stevensons' ring. Greta appeared at the door of the dining room and announced that the call was from Mark for Maureen.

"May I take it?" she asked. "I'm finished eating."

"Yes, this time, but tell Mark that normally you can't take calls during the dinner hour," Mother said.

Mark quickly announced that since his father was handling the estate of a man, he'd discovered the perfect automobile for Mrs. Hoag. Mark seemed disappointed that Maureen already knew his news and that her father was going to speak to Mrs. Hoag that evening.

"Call me after he gets back," Mark said.

"I may have to wait and tell you at school," Maureen said. "I must hurry to a WCTU meeting with Mother." And hurry she did. She changed dresses and scurried down the stairs where Mother waited.

Father drove them in the automobile to the meeting held at the president's home.

"Are you ready?" Mother asked, as they walked up to the house.

"Yes, Mother. I'll do my best to remember."

"That's all I want from you, Maureen. You doing your best."

There was already a roomful of women, and Maureen acknowledged introductions by a slight bow of her head and a "very pleased to meet you," as Mother had taught her.

After the president called the meeting to order, Maureen listened to reports of the various committees. Women had sat outside a barroom and recorded the names of the men who went inside for a drink. That usually made men uncomfortable, so they would avoid that place in the future. Because of lost business from the WCTU's activities, five establishments so far had closed down.

When it was time for the committee report on the teaching at school, Mother stood and introduced Maureen.

Maureen walked to the front of the room and swallowed hard. Staring at a portrait on the back wall of the sitting room, she held up her hand and pointed to each finger as she recited,

"One, two, three, four, five fingers on every little hand.
Listen while they speak to us; be sure we understand.
1. THERE IS A DRINK THAT NEVER HARMS. *It will make*
    us strong.
2. THERE IS A DRINK THAT NEVER ALARMS. *Some drinks*
    make people wicked.
3. *A* DRINK THAT KEEPS OUR SENSES RIGHT. *There are*
    drinks that will take away our senses.
4. *A* DRINK THAT MAKES OUR FACES BRIGHT. *We should*
    never touch the drinks that will put evil into our hearts
    and spoil our faces.
5. GOD GIVES US THE ONLY DRINK—'TIS PURE, COLD
    WATER.*"

The ladies applauded, and Maureen took her seat with a sigh of relief. Her mother patted her on the knee. "That was very nice, Maureen."

"Thank you, Mother."

For the rest of the meeting, Maureen let her mind drift to Mrs.

Hoag and the job and the automobile.

"She is out of hand," Mother said, and Maureen's attention came back to the meeting. "We aren't out to destroy property, merely to shut down the establishments and get rid of evil alcohol."

"She's getting her name known around the country. It may help our cause," the president said.

"But she is getting more violent," another member said. "I don't like her being associated with the WCTU."

"Who?" Maureen whispered.

"Carrie Nation," her mother whispered back. "I'll explain later."

The members didn't decide anything about Carrie Nation, but after they concluded their business and were drinking tea and socializing, Mother described the crusader's actions.

"At first she went to a saloon in Kansas and smashed a keg of whiskey. Then she used any weapon available, even rocks thrown at mirrors and windows. Now she's carrying a hatchet, and she splinters furniture and breaks bottles and shatters kegs everywhere she goes. People will think all of us WCTU members are as mad as she is."

"You think she's crazy?"

"I don't know, but I've heard she flies into rages, and her family has a history of insanity."

"Oh," Maureen said and drank another sip of her tea. If insanity ran in families, then she should ask Mrs. Hoag to tell her more about her family in Ireland. And if Mrs. Hoag's family were normal, Maureen could tell the others at school that Mrs. Hoag wasn't crazy after all, even if she did think she knew President Roosevelt.

CHAPTER 6

Maureen's Secret

"Mrs. Hoag's buying the automobile," Maureen told Mark the next day at school. "Father said she didn't even need to see it. She's taking his word about it."

"Now I know two people who have automobiles," Mark said. "I wish my family had one."

"Uncle Albert will buy one someday," Maureen said in an effort to make him feel better. "Besides, your family is so big, all of you couldn't fit into one. You'd need one with three backseats, and who would ever think of making an automobile that big?"

Mark laughed. "That *would* be funny looking."

Maureen was glad that wistful note was out of his voice, for she didn't think it likely that his family would get an automobile any time soon. She'd overheard Father say to Mother that Uncle Albert had a lot of mouths to feed. Five children took a lot of clothing and shoes, too.

Since the Stevensons had adopted her, they had showered her with new clothes. Maureen lacked no essential item. She had protested to Mother that she didn't need so many dresses. Although she didn't say so, she didn't want to be a burden to them. But Mother had insisted that Maureen have several dresses and three pairs of shoes.

Three pairs of shoes. Mama would have thought that was unnecessary since Maureen would outgrow them before they wore out.

She looked down at the toe of the brown shoe peeking out from under her skirt and was thankful she had been adopted instead of sent to an orphanage like some of the schoolgirls had whispered might happen to her.

Today the girls were still friendly and full of curious questions about Mrs. Hoag. As before, they gathered around Maureen and Mark outside the school before the afternoon session began.

"She's not crazy," Maureen told them. "Mother calls her eccentric, but that just means she has odd ways. She's been all over the West to Dakota and in the East to New York, and China and Africa and Europe."

"You've been in Europe, too," Mark said. "Ireland's in Europe. And you lived in New York."

"Does that make you eccentric, too?" Sarah asked and laughed.

Mark looked taken aback, as if he hadn't meant to put Maureen in that kind of light.

"It means she's been places and done things we haven't," Mark said. "Have you ever been out of Minnesota?"

Sarah smirked. "I've taken the train to Iowa to visit my aunt."

"Well, Maureen's crossed the ocean on a big ship and ridden the train across the country to here."

"So what? That makes her an immigrant," Sarah said.

Maureen stepped back as if she'd been struck. The way Sarah said the word was the same as saying she was beneath them. Oh, she had known that feeling before, when she'd first started school and seen the division between the servant class and the wealthy class. But at that moment it was a slap to her mama and papa, and Maureen wanted to reach out and strike Sarah. She closed her eyes a moment and remembered the Sunday school lesson from the week before on turning the other cheek. She swallowed hard and didn't say a word.

"Mrs. Hoag says traveling lets you see places you never dreamed of and lets you see people doing things you would never see except in magazine drawings and pictures," Mark said.

"But Mrs. Hoag is eccentric," Sarah said.

A teacher rang the bell, and the students lined up to go back inside the school.

"Sorry," Mark said to Maureen before he took his place in line with his class.

The rest of the afternoon, Maureen kept her head lowered, with her eyes on her desk or her papers. She didn't raise her hand to answer any questions, even though history was her favorite subject, and she didn't talk to anyone when the students worked in small groups on a science experiment.

After school, Maureen walked home alone. She wished it was a workday and she could talk to Mrs. Hoag more about the time when she came to America. As Maureen neared Mrs. Hoag's mansion, she made a sudden decision and turned down the drive.

"Why, Maureen, it's only Wednesday," Mrs. Hoag said when she answered the door. "I didn't expect you until tomorrow."

"I know. I just wanted to ask you something." Maureen didn't know where she found the courage to face Mrs. Hoag alone. One moment she thought the old woman was crazy saying she heard voices and knew President Roosevelt, and the next moment she found Mrs. Hoag as a link to her own country and in a strange way as a link to her mama.

"Come in," Mrs. Hoag said. She wore a dark blue dress and had her hair pinned up. She led the way to the Oriental Room. "Please sit down. Now what is troubling you, Maureen?"

Mrs. Hoag seemed different today, concerned, no odd glint in her eye or cackling laughter—just normal. She could have been like any of the ladies at the WCTU meeting.

Maureen didn't know how to start. She couldn't ask how Mrs. Hoag had stood people looking down on her because she wasn't born in America. She couldn't ask her if people made fun of her accent or her ways. She took a deep breath and just began. "You've been an immigrant for a long time."

"No," Mrs. Hoag said. "I'm not an immigrant. I'm a citizen."

"You are?"

"Of course. Franklin's mother insisted upon it, and I'm glad she did." As if talking to herself, Mrs. Hoag said in a quieter voice, "I'm surprised Nadine Stevenson hasn't talked to you about it. Maybe she thought it was too early and would take away your identity."

Hope rose in Maureen. Could she become a citizen, too?

"How old do you have to be?"

Mrs. Hoag smiled. "No age limit, but there's a time limit. Tell me again when you came to this country."

"When I was almost three, and I'll be eleven in July."

"That's plenty long. I think the requirement is five years, but the law may have changed since I took the oath. You need to swear to uphold the government and obey its laws. And you can't be a criminal or insane," she said with a laugh, "but I can vouch for you there. If you'd like, I'll ask Sidney Orr to look up the laws and see what steps you need to be taking to become a citizen." Her voice softened. "Why is this important to you?" she asked.

Maureen explained about the girls at school.

"I'm thinking some of them are not long off the boat themselves. Maybe second-generation Americans. They shouldn't be so high and mighty. Not that I haven't seen it before. Franklin's father's family had been here since before the Revolution, but his mother's family was another thing. Her family came over from Italy a few months before she was born, so you might say she crossed the ocean, too, in her mother's womb. She was proud to be American-born, and she never confided the story of her birth to me, but Franklin's father told him. I never held it against her or for her. We all have different things that make us proud. Maybe her family was looked down on, so she held her head up because she was a native."

Mrs. Hoag reached over and lifted Maureen's chin with her finger. "And you, child, are going to lift your head up high, too."

"Yes, ma'am," Maureen said with a much lighter heart than when she'd knocked on Mrs. Hoag's door. "I'd best be going. Mother will wonder why I'm late from school."

"I'll see you tomorrow," Mrs. Hoag said and waved good-bye from the doorway.

Maureen hurried home and found Mother in the parlor with another lady from the WCTU. Although she wanted to talk to her then, Maureen went to her room.

She picked up the picture of her mama from the dresser and stared at it. "Should I become a citizen, Mama? Did you ever think of doing it?"

Instead of starting her homework, Maureen stared out the window, waiting to see the guest leave. When the front door finally closed with a thump, she ran downstairs and burst into the parlor.

"Mother," she said as she stood in front of her mother's chair. "I want to be a citizen."

Her mother looked surprised, but she nodded her head. "Good."

"Why didn't my mama become a citizen? Mrs. Hoag says it takes being in this country only five years."

"You've talked to Mrs. Hoag?"

"She'll be having Sidney Orr see what the laws are about it. But my mama?"

"I'm not sure, Maureen. I think she felt it was disloyal to your papa or maybe giving up too much of her heritage, but I'm glad you've decided to do it. But why now?"

Maureen explained about Sarah's comments. When she was through, Mother reached out and hugged her.

"Sometimes people are mean-spirited, but you did the right thing in turning the other cheek and not saying anything hateful back to Sarah. I'll talk to Mrs. Hoag and see what she finds out so that we can file the necessary forms."

"Thank you, Mother. I'm not going to tell the girls at school until I'm a citizen, but I might tell Mark."

"Fine. For now it will be our family secret," Mother said.

The next day after school as Maureen and Mark were walking to Mrs. Hoag's, Maureen shared her secret of becoming a citizen. "But you can't tell anyone. Promise?"

"Promise," Mark said.

As before, Mrs. Hoag opened the door as they climbed the porch steps.

"Are you ready to work?" she asked.

"Western Room, here we come," Mark said.

They cataloged the rest of the statues that day and then moved into the French Room, which was also on the third floor. The artwork was different here. The paintings weren't as real-life looking as those in the Western Room.

"This looks like scribbles," Mark said.

"Stand over here to look at it," Mrs. Hoag said. "Then you'll see what the artist saw."

"It's a horse race," Maureen said from across the room.

"Exactly. Manet painted *The Races at Longchamp.* It's supposed to be seen like you would see it. Your eye couldn't focus on the horses and the people watching it, so he gave the impression of the people without drawing faces."

"I like faces," Mark said.

"That's a different style of art," Mrs. Hoag said. "Look at this one."

Maureen squinted her eyes to make out the name of the artist. "Is this the same man? Manet?"

"No, this is Monet. That's an *o* instead of an *a,* but the two artists were friends. When I met Monet, he was on a boat that he had fixed up into an artist's studio. He said an artist should only paint nature from nature itself. And he had to paint fast, because clouds could cover the sun and make the lighting different or wind could break the reflection of the water. He was an odd fellow, but quite likable."

So Mrs. Hoag knew this man, too. *Or at least she says she does,* Maureen thought. Could she possibly know President Roosevelt and Frederic Remington and Monet?

"These men called themselves Impressionists. Franklin was like you, Mark. He liked the faces to have eyes and noses and hair."

"I like Remington's statues the best," Maureen said. "When we finish today, could I come back with Father's camera and take a picture of *The Wicked Pony*? I told Father about it, and he'd like to see it."

"He should have mentioned it when he came by today with the automobile," Mrs. Hoag said. "I would have shown it to him."

"You got the electric?" Mark asked, excitement in his voice.

"Shall I take you two for a ride to Maureen's house to get the camera?" Mrs. Hoag asked.

"Oh yes," Mark said.

"Then let's finish our work for today and we shall try out the Road-Wagon."

They worked well together for the rest of the time. Mark read off the name of the artist, and Maureen stood across the room and described the work. Mrs. Hoag gave more fascinating history about each one as she wrote long notes, but Maureen didn't know if it was all true or not.

"The time's up," Mrs. Hoag finally said. "Shall we go get that camera?"

With elaborate care, Mrs. Hoag donned a driving hat with a billowing veil and a long coat. "I went to George Dayton's department store this morning," she said, "and purchased the proper attire for my electric."

She led them out the back door to the carriage house, where the electric had been recharging. Mark claimed the spot next to Mrs. Hoag, which left Maureen on the outside.

"It doesn't have to be cranked," Mark said.

"No. It works off a battery," Mrs. Hoag said. She started the

Road-Wagon, then pulled the steering tiller to the left. The car moved to the right.

"You have to move it the opposite way," Mark said.

"I need some practice," Mrs. Hoag said. "I told Theodore Stevenson that I could manage, and manage I will. In my younger days I drove a horse and buggy all over Minneapolis."

Maureen refrained from repeating what she'd told Mark, that driving a horse and an automobile were two different things.

The vehicle lurched forward, then the ride smoothed out even though they only moved a few inches each second. Mrs. Hoag wildly moved the stick back and forth, trying to avoid the bird feeders sticking up in the backyard.

Finally they reached the street. Mrs. Hoag made the Road-Wagon go faster, not nearly the pace that Father drove his automobile, but faster than she'd been going in the yard.

At one point, she took her hands off the tiller and reached up to adjust her hat.

"Mrs. Hoag!" Mark shouted. The Road-Wagon veered dangerously to one side as the right wheel went off the road and skimmed along the ditch. Mark grabbed the tiller and pulled it sharply toward him.

Maureen was thrown against the door, which swung open. She screamed and clung to it, dangling in midair until the force of the turning wheels made the door swing back against the body of the car, and the automobile found solid road beneath all four wheels.

Mrs. Hoag stopped the automobile in the street and patted her chest with her hand. "Oh my! Oh my!"

"You have to watch what you're doing," Mark said in a voice

that sounded like Father's when he was explaining driving to Mark.

Mrs. Hoag looked sharply at him. "I can do this. That was a temporary lapse." She stared straight at the road and kept her hand on the tiller. She made a U-turn in the street while Maureen ran into the house and got Father's Brownie camera. Maureen climbed into the automobile again, glad the house was only two blocks away.

Mrs. Hoag maneuvered the Road-Wagon back to her house and inched it into the carriage house.

"That was a wild ride," Mark said. "I liked it."

"I just need a little practice," Mrs. Hoag said.

They climbed the stairs to the third floor, and Maureen took pictures of two of Remington's statues.

"When Father has these developed, I'll give a picture to you," Maureen said.

"That would be fine. Now, would you like a ride home?" Mrs. Hoag asked.

"Thank you, but we'll walk," Maureen said.

CHAPTER 7

The Missing Statue

"Father, would you give Mrs. Hoag some instructions on driving her electric?" Maureen asked at dinner that night.

"She told me she was fine with it when I took it over," Father said. "The literature about the car said even a child could handle it."

Maureen told them about the wild two-block ride.

"Theodore, I don't want Maureen riding with Mrs. Hoag if she's unsafe," Mother said.

"Oh, it wasn't unsafe," Maureen hurriedly assured her. "We weren't going at all fast. I could have walked here faster than riding in her Road-Wagon. Please don't say I can't ride with her, Mother. I merely wanted Father to give her some instruction. . .without her knowing it."

"How's this? I'll call and ask if I can go for a ride in her electric. Then when she's showing me how it works, I'll give her a few hints."

"Oh, Father, that would be wonderful," Maureen said and beamed at him.

True to his promise, Father called Mrs. Hoag and arranged for a drive the next day after he got home from the bank. Mrs. Hoag told Maureen and Mark all about it on Saturday when they were working.

"I'll drive you home today, and you can see how much I've improved. I told you I just needed a little practice."

Maureen thanked her but said they would walk so the electric could keep charging.

They worked in the French Room again and finished cataloging the paintings and statues. There weren't nearly as many as in the huge Western Room.

"That's all that's on the top floor," Mrs. Hoag said. "Of course, the ballroom takes up most of the space. The French Room was used as a ladies' powder room when Franklin's parents lived here."

"This is an old house," Mark said.

"It sure is. Franklin grew up here. Hoags have always lived here. But the end is near since we didn't have any children and Franklin was an only child. There are no more Hoags left. Only me," she said in a sad voice.

"I like this house," Maureen said.

"Do you think it has any hidden rooms or secret passageways?" Mark asked.

Mrs. Hoag smiled, and the warmth of it reached her eyes. "Would a secret staircase do?"

"Do you really have a secret staircase?" Mark asked.

As an answer, Mrs. Hoag walked over to the wall by the French Room fireplace. She pushed against a dark wood panel, and it swung inward. She reached inside and pulled out a lantern.

"I keep a lantern at the top and the bottom of the staircase. When Franklin had the house wired for electricity, he decided not to tell the workmen about this staircase. It wouldn't be a secret if everyone knew about it."

Maureen had thought it odd that there wasn't a painting hung in the three-foot area next to the fireplace, because the other walls were packed with artwork. Now she understood why. If a painting were hung there, it would fall when the secret panel moved.

Mrs. Hoag lit the lantern. "Want to see what's in here?"

There was no question about that. Mark rushed to Mrs. Hoag's side, and Maureen followed. Mrs. Hoag carried the lantern and let the light play all around the narrow winding stairs.

"What was this used for?" Mark asked.

"I don't know. Maybe it was built as a whim. Franklin said he had fun playing in it when he was young."

They followed the steep stairs down to the second floor. Mrs. Hoag pushed on another secret panel that opened into a bedroom. They peeked in, then closed the panel.

Mrs. Hoag led the way to the first floor. She pushed open another panel and stepped out of the staircase.

"We're in the Oriental Room!" Mark exclaimed as he and Maureen followed Mrs. Hoag.

Maureen closed the panel door beside the fireplace. "I couldn't pick it out if I didn't know it was there." She moved it back and forth. It opened easily without a squeak.

"Mark, would you go back up these stairs and hang the light at the top?" Mrs. Hoag asked.

As soon as she closed the panel behind him, Mrs. Hoag turned to Maureen. "I spoke with Sidney about your citizenship. You only have to fill out some forms and swear allegiance to the United States. He said the government is getting ready to make some changes in the naturalization policy. There are some senators who want to make it harder to become a citizen, so you'd best be doing this soon. Your mother called, and I told her all of that. She said she would pursue it immediately."

"Thank you, Mrs. Hoag. I told Mark about it, but I'm not telling anyone else until I'm a citizen."

"Quiet, be quiet." Ruthie waddled into the room. "Be quiet."

"Shush yourself," Mark said with a laugh as he joined them in the Oriental Room. "Are we done for the day?"

Mrs. Hoag nodded and fetched her handbag. She took out two envelopes and handed one to Maureen and one to Mark. "That's for the first week's work. I'm thinking we got a lot done this week. Now, next week, we'll be working on the second floor. And next Saturday I have a surprise for you. I'd like you to come in the morning, like you did today, but ask your parents if you can stay to lunch and not be home until late afternoon."

Mark said it would be fine, and Maureen could almost see him adding up the extra money he'd make.

They waved good-bye with a promise of returning after school on Tuesday to start the African Room.

Father had said he'd help Mark work on his brother's bicycle that afternoon, so Maureen had put off plans to go roller-skating until the next Saturday. Now that they'd be working all day for Mrs. Hoag, that would be off, too, but that was all right. Since Sarah had called her an immigrant in that superior voice, Maureen hadn't wanted to be around her and her friends. And she certainly didn't want to go to the roller rink without Mark. He was her friend, her protector, and the best cousin anyone could ask for.

Early that morning, Uncle Albert had brought Mark and Calvin's bicycle over in a hired wagon so that Mark and Father could fix it. Mark had bought the parts he needed with Mrs. Hoag's reward money.

After the noon meal, he and Father worked on the bicycle, putting on a new wheel and straightening the bent fender. Maureen watched as they oiled the friction points and polished the metal, then Mark climbed on and rode up and down the drive.

"It works like a dream, Uncle Theodore," he called as he flew by, his feet moving fast on the pedals.

"Maureen, it's time you learned to ride a bicycle," Father said. "You may be a bit small for Nadine's bicycle, but I imagine you can manage it."

From the carriage house he wheeled out a woman's two-wheeler. Maureen straddled the bicycle and put her feet where Father said to. He held onto the seat and ran behind her as she pedaled along. When he let go, the bicycle wobbled, and down Maureen went.

"It's a matter of practice," Father said. "Much like Mrs. Hoag with her electric." He explained about balance and brakes and speed, and then they tried it again and again. Each time Father let go, Maureen fell.

She was ready to give up when Father ran behind her for a longer distance than he had before. Suddenly, she was halfway down the drive.

"You're doing it!" Mark yelled. "You're riding!"

Maureen glanced behind her and saw that Father had let go at his regular spot. That was all she needed to fall once again, but now she had the confidence that she could ride, and she tried it again and again until it felt comfortable leaning this way and that.

"I'm riding!" she called. "I'm riding!"

All the next week, Maureen rode the bicycle to school. So did Mark, and together they rode to Mrs. Hoag's for their job during the week and on Saturday morning.

"I brought the pictures of the Remingtons," Maureen announced early Saturday morning. They had come out fairly well. If there had been better lighting in the ballroom, they would have been better. "Could I look in the Western Room for a minute?"

"Of course. Meet us back on the second floor."

Mark climbed the secret staircase to the second floor, as he'd been doing all week. Maureen climbed the main staircase to the third floor. She carried the pictures to compare to the statue of *The Wicked Pony*. The way that horse bucked, standing only on its two front feet, fascinated her. Father had said Remington was an outstanding artist, and maybe he would get one of his sculptures. If he did, she'd like him to get one like this one.

She opened the door to the ballroom and hurried to the third table in the row next to the windows, but the statue wasn't there. In its place was a horse standing on all four legs. She looked around but didn't see *The Wicked Pony*.

Maureen quickly made her way down to the second floor, where Mark and Mrs. Hoag were already in the African Room.

"Where did you move *The Wicked Pony*?" she asked.

"I haven't moved it," Mrs. Hoag said.

"Then it's gone," Maureen said. "Come look."

The threesome climbed the stairs, and they all looked at the table where the Remington was kept.

"It's always been there. Franklin put it there himself. He liked the way the light came in from the windows and added life to that horse."

They started at one end of the room and looked at each statue. Not one of them was *The Wicked Pony*.

"Did we imagine that statue?" Mrs. Hoag said. "Is this my

mind playing tricks on me again?"

Maureen held out the picture. "We didn't imagine it. Someone took that statue and put another one in its place so you wouldn't notice it was gone."

"I wonder if any of the others are gone," Mark said.

Mrs. Hoag got her cataloging papers for the Western Room, and they went piece by piece around the room. Soon they found another switch. Two paintings had been taken and others hung in their places.

"The burglar is very selective," Mrs. Hoag said. "And he's very clever. If we weren't cataloging these items, I would never have noticed that something was missing."

"What about the other rooms?" Mark asked.

They checked the catalog against the objects in the French and African Rooms and found each item in its place.

"I can't be sure about the uncataloged rooms," Mrs. Hoag said. "We never made a complete list before. We just estimated the worth of the items for insurance purposes."

"Do you think the thief is the same person who took your handbag?" Maureen asked.

"I'm thinking it's the same thief, but how could he get in? Bertha and I lock this house up tight. I'll be having a word with Bertha right now. I also need to call the police and report this," Mrs. Hoag said and left Mark and Maureen to go downstairs.

"If you didn't have that picture, Mrs. Hoag would think she was imagining things," Mark said.

"Quiet, be quiet," Ruthie said as she waddled into the room.

"Imagining things. . .like the voices?" Maureen said. "Ruthie, who should be quiet?"

"Quiet, be quiet," Ruthie repeated.

"I'm thinking that Ruthie knows who has taken these things," Maureen said. "There must be more than one thief. The voices Mrs. Hoag hears are the thieves talking to each other."

She heard Mrs. Hoag coming up the stairs, her footsteps loud on the wooden steps. "Could footsteps be the noises she hears at night?"

"Bertha doesn't know anything about the Remington," Mrs. Hoag said. "She doesn't even go into the rooms where we have the artwork. Until now I've not been worrying about keeping them dusted."

"Did you call the police?" Mark asked.

"I did, but I'll have to wait a while for one to come to the house to write a report. Many are already in St. Paul helping out there with the parade. Oh," she said and covered her mouth with her hand. "I didn't mean to mention that."

"We've talked at school about the parade," Maureen said. "If we weren't working for you, we'd go and see President Roosevelt." She hadn't wanted to mention it, because she didn't want to force Mrs. Hoag to acknowledge that she didn't know the important man.

"We *are* going," Mrs. Hoag said. "That's my surprise for today. Let's work a wee bit on the African Room, and then we'll go to St. Paul for a nice meal at a special restaurant and see Theodore."

So she calls him by his first name now, Maureen thought. What would she do when he didn't acknowledge her presence at the parade? How would Mrs. Hoag react?

Cataloging artifacts in the African Room was slow work. Although Mark and Maureen described what they saw, they didn't know the significance of each item. Most were primitive, and their significance and their countries and the tribes were unknown to Maureen. But each one sparked a long story from Mrs. Hoag.

Maureen cringed as she dusted the animal skulls and carved wooden figures. Who had boiled the skin off these skulls and arranged them in this specific pattern? A witch doctor? Just last week Mother had read aloud an article from the National Geographic Society about African tribes. They had talked about missionaries going to darkest Africa to enlighten the tribes about Jesus. That continent was not a place Maureen wanted to go.

The threesome worked for another couple hours in the African Room. Then they loaded up in the electric, and Mrs. Hoag drove them across the bridge to St. Paul.

The streets were crowded with people. Mark squeezed the horn as Mrs. Hoag zigzagged between people. The automobile wasn't going very fast, but Maureen held on for dear life and took a big breath when Mrs. Hoag finally stopped the car beside a downtown restaurant.

"We'll eat here, then get a good spot to see the parade," she said.

Maureen and Mark exchanged a look, and Maureen knew he was thinking the same thing that she was. How long would Mrs. Hoag keep up the pretense of knowing President Roosevelt?

Their meal was delicious. Mrs. Hoag ordered chicken fricassee for all of them with corn on the cob and mashed potatoes. For dessert they had ice cream and cake, the most expensive item on the dessert menu. It would have taken Maureen an hour and a half of work at Mrs. Hoag's just to pay for dessert, but Mrs. Hoag acted as if the price didn't matter.

Once they finished eating, they left the electric where it was parked and walked to the parade route. People milled everywhere and stood five and six deep along East Sixth Street.

Maureen was relieved to see the crowd. If the three of them couldn't get close to the street, then President Roosevelt couldn't see them, and Mrs. Hoag wouldn't be embarrassed when he passed them by without a word.

They kept walking and finally found a place where they could squeeze in, but Mrs. Hoag said they must go one block farther. Finally they reached the spot she was seeking, and Mark and Maureen stood close together in front of Mrs. Hoag, right behind a row of policemen who were keeping people out of the street.

"Here they come," someone yelled, and word was passed down the long row of spectators.

A band led the procession. Next came military men in uniform and veterans of the Spanish-American War carrying a banner and the American flag.

Then in the first open carriage, waving his hat, sat President Theodore Roosevelt. He looked exactly like the picture of him that hung in the hallway at school.

"Theodore!" Mrs. Hoag shouted as his carriage drew across from them. "Theodore, it's Lillian Hoag!" she called above the applause.

The president must have heard her, for he turned in their direction and scanned the crowd.

"Theodore, it's Lillian Hoag." She waved with both arms.

The president leaned forward and spoke to the driver, who pulled up on the team of horses.

"Lillian," he shouted and climbed out of the carriage and walked directly toward them. The policemen in front of them parted to let Mrs. Hoag through. She hugged the president, then waved at Maureen and Mark to join her in the street.

"Mr. President, I'd like you to meet Maureen Stevenson and Mark Bowman."

As if in a daze, Maureen reached for his outstretched hand.

CHAPTER 8

Easter Traditions

"Let me shake the hand that shook the hand of President Roosevelt," Uncle Albert said to Maureen before Sunday dinner. The Stevensons had gone to the Bowmans' home straight after church and were in the front parlor awaiting the call to eat.

Maureen laughed as Mark's father grabbed her hand. He always wore a smile, and she had liked him the first time she'd met him.

"Did you shake Mark's hand, too?"

"Over and over," he said with a laugh. "That boy still can't calm down."

"My heart's still beating double-time, too," Maureen said. She had a hard time comprehending that she had actually met the president. Even more startling had been the revelation that Mrs. Hoag knew the man. That story about her sitting on the front porch of his ranch house was true. The president had mentioned their time in Dakota. Did that mean her other stories about famous people were also true?

"That Mrs. Hoag is quite a lady," Uncle Albert said.

"She said she'd sent a telegram to President Roosevelt telling him that we would be at the parade right at that spot," Maureen said. "He must have been looking for us."

"Imagine that," Mother said. "Mrs. Hoag was very kind to

include Maureen and Mark. I knew she was a civic-minded woman, but recently I asked the ladies on my committee a few questions about her."

She leaned toward Uncle Albert as if confiding in him. "I learned she and her husband were instrumental in getting the new library, the art gallery, and the natural science museum all in that building on Hennepin Avenue. She was a great patron of the arts; and from what Maureen tells me about her worldwide collections, she's still very interested in the fine arts."

"I'm glad Mark and Maureen are getting her out of that house. Mark's full of her driving that electric," Uncle Albert said.

"Everything is ready," Aunt Annie announced, and the two families made their way into the dining room.

Mark's brother and sisters, his parents, Maureen, and her new parents crowded around the table, and Uncle Albert asked the blessing, remembering that today they celebrated Palm Sunday and Jesus' triumphal entry into Jerusalem. After the final amen, which was echoed around the table, there was no shortage of conversation. Calvin told Mark that his old bicycle looked better than it ever had, and Eva and Annette were kind as could be to Maureen. After dinner the older ones talked among themselves, leaving Mark and Maureen and Sophie to play croquet outside in the spring sunshine.

All too soon, it was time for the Stevensons to go home, and Maureen waved at her extended family as Father drove them home in his automobile.

Back in her own room, Maureen picked up the picture of her mama. "It's Palm Sunday, Mama. I guess we won't have your Easter cake this year. And we didn't have Mothering Sunday last week. I didn't give Mother a present. It would seem wrong, some-how, her not being Irish."

Tears blurred her vision as she looked at Mama's smiling face. "I have a new family now, but things are so different. Why do things keep changing so? I do what Mother says. I pray for things to be easier, but some days I feel a great weight on my heart, and I miss you so." Maureen gave into the feeling of despair and cried in the loneliness of her room. Then she dried her tears and went back downstairs to be with Mother and Father.

It rained on Monday, and the students stayed indoors during the noon break. Mark had told everyone he saw that he had shaken the hand of President Roosevelt, and students stood in line to shake the very hand that had touched the president. Some of the girls made their way over to Maureen, but Sarah led those who thought it was silly to think there was some remnant of the president on her hand after two days.

"Unless she hasn't washed her hand," Sarah said, and the other girls in her little group snickered.

Maureen did her best to ignore them. Why was Sarah out to make fun of her? She couldn't figure out a reason.

On Tuesday after school, Mark charged into Mrs. Hoag's secret staircase, holding the lantern in front of him.

"Maureen! Come here." His voice was muffled since he'd just shut the secret entrance door, but Maureen heard him. She pushed open the panel in the Oriental Room and looked inside. Mark hadn't started up the steps.

"What is it?" she asked.

"Look!" He pointed to the first step. "Here's a footprint. Some-body's been here."

"Where?"

"Right here." He held the lantern so the light fell on the step. "It's only half a footprint."

"It just looks like mud to me," she said. "Is it from your boots?"

"No," he said, although Maureen saw some mud clinging to his left boot. "It's dried mud. Somebody else has used this staircase. And he used it last night after the rain. I'll bet it was the thief."

"Or Mrs. Hoag. Or her housekeeper," Maureen suggested.

Mark held the lantern up high, but there was only the one partial print.

Mrs. Hoag said she'd not been on the stairs and that Bertha didn't even know about the secret staircase.

"Let's check again for missing items," Mark said. They hurried to the Western Room and compared the art with the catalog. Nothing had been replaced by inferior artwork.

Maureen walked over by the windows and looked down toward the creek. On the near side of the creek, where the bank formed a short bluff and the creek came closest to the house, a figure crouched and appeared to be pounding something. As if he felt someone staring at him, he stood and looked up through the bare limbs of the trees toward the house. Maureen stepped away from the windows. Surely it was just a boy like Mark who liked playing by the creek.

Maureen slipped over by the paintings and leaned against the wall.

"Nothing's missing," Mrs. Hoag said. "Let's get on to the African Room. We have a lot of work to do in there."

Maureen pushed away from the wall and felt it move behind her.

"Mark! Mrs. Hoag!" She was almost too frightened to turn around, but she forced herself to look back. There was an opening, just a sliver. Was there another secret staircase here that Mrs. Hoag hadn't mentioned?

Mark ran over to the spot. The small, movable panel wasn't a foot wide. He pushed the door all the way and stuck his head inside the space. "It's a room." It was actually the size of a small closet, about two yards square.

"My goodness," Mrs. Hoag said. "I didn't know it was there!"

Mark slid the door shut, then tried to reopen it but couldn't.

Maureen showed them how she had pushed off from the wall with her left hand. It took a few minutes to position herself in the same way so that she found the spring-loaded spot that made the door open.

"Hmm. This house holds many secrets," Mrs. Hoag said. "Franklin never mentioned this place. I wonder if he knew."

Mrs. Hoag tried it, and they opened and shut the door that hid the secret closet.

"I wonder if there are other hidden spaces," Maureen said.

She and Mark inched their way along the two walls of paintings but found no other area that would give under pressure. When she ended up by the wall of windows, Maureen glanced outside and noted that the figure was no longer by the creek. But was there something red in the place where the person had stood—or was she seeing things? She decided to look at that spot after they finished their work.

They checked over the French Room and found nothing amiss, then got to work on the odd relics in the African Room.

This room was taking forever to catalog. Mrs. Hoag was explaining another of those pieces with many skulls stuck together when a sharp cry from below stopped her in midsentence.

"Bertha!" Mrs. Hoag exclaimed. "Children, run and see what's wrong."

Maureen and Mark flew downstairs, while Mrs. Hoag followed at a more sedate pace.

Maureen found the servant in the kitchen holding a bloody towel to her hand. She had never met Bertha before, but she wasn't surprised to see an older woman who couldn't be too many years younger than Mrs. Hoag.

"Where are you hurt?" Maureen cried and rushed to Bertha's side and grabbed the towel. The sight of Bertha's cut forefinger and thumb made her stomach lurch, and she wasn't sure what she should do to help.

"Get another towel and a chair." Mrs. Hoag had arrived and took charge. "What happened, Bertha?"

Mark moved a chair to the counter, and Bertha sank into it and held her hand over the sink. Blood oozed from her cuts.

"I was cutting the fruit when the knife slipped," Bertha said. "Trying to cut too many at a time, and I pushed too hard."

Mrs. Hoag held another towel over the cuts. "Once we stop the bleeding, we will dress it. Maureen, there's gauze and ointment in the bathroom through there."

Maureen scurried away and found the medical supplies. When she returned, she stood out of the way while Mrs. Hoag held the towel on Bertha's wounds. Maureen glanced away from the bloody sight and gazed at the center counter in the large kitchen that held almonds and sultanas, currants and raisins.

"Are you making simnel cake?" she asked with hope in her heart.

"Now what kind of Irish woman would I be without a simnel cake at Easter?" Mrs. Hoag asked.

"I used to help Mama with the chopping," Maureen said wistfully.

Mrs. Hoag looked hard at Maureen, then gave her attention to her servant. She removed the bloody towel and replaced it with a fresh one. "The bleeding has slowed," she said. "Mark, run upstairs and close up the African Room so Ruthie can't get in there. Maureen, would you mind chopping the fruit?"

Maureen quickly grabbed the sharp knife and started to work.

"Go easy, now. We don't want two cooks with cuts," Mrs. Hoag said. "Why don't you call Nadine and see if you can stay here for dinner and help finish the cake?"

Maureen couldn't reach the phone fast enough to place the call.

Her words tumbled out when her mother answered. "May I please stay and help Mrs. Hoag with her simnel cake? She makes one every year just like Mama did. And Bertha cut her fingers, and she needs me to chop fruit."

"Slow down, Maureen," Mother said. "Is this the Easter cake?"

"Yes." Maureen held her breath while her mother considered her request.

"I think it's fine that you help Mrs. Hoag," Mother said. "When do you think you'll be home?"

They worked out the details, and then Maureen turned her attention to chopping. "Are the almonds ground up for the marzipan?" she asked a white-faced Bertha, who was holding still while Mrs. Hoag bandaged her fingers.

"Over by the stove," Bertha said.

Maureen smiled. Mama always warmed them before she added the egg white and kneaded the mixture to ice the cake and made a firm paste for the marzipan eggs that would decorate the top.

Mrs. Hoag helped Bertha to her room, and then she returned to the kitchen.

"Mark, do you want to help us with the cake?" she asked.

He looked unsure.

"This is an Irish tradition," Maureen explained with a big smile. "Mama said that her mama before her made simnel cake and her mama before her and on and on forever. Now I get to do it, too, even though I'm adopted in America."

"Do you have another knife?" he asked.

While Mrs. Hoag made the buttery batter, Maureen and Mark chopped the dried fruits. Soon the cake was ready for the oven. While it baked, they made the marzipan out of the ground almonds, sugar, and egg whites.

"Mark, you can shape the eggs out of this stiffer mixture," Mrs. Hoag said, then added another egg white to the almond paste that she and Maureen kneaded.

"Do you serve it with warm apricot jam?" Maureen asked.

"Never have," Mrs. Hoag said. "That's the thing about traditions. We can each put our own touches to them. We used peach preserves in the Cooney home. That was my name before I married Franklin. Lillian Cooney."

"Are there any Cooneys left in Ireland?" Maureen asked.

"Oh, yes. I have a brother and several nieces and nephews in the old country. I saw them a few years ago when Franklin and I went to Europe."

"Are they all fine?" Maureen asked, remembering her plan to discover if Mrs. Hoag had any insane relatives like Carrie Nation did. Talk at school about Mrs. Hoag being crazy had lessened now that she'd proven she actually knew President Roosevelt, but still it would be good to learn more about her.

Mrs. Hoag had an odd look on her face. "My relatives are fine. All healthy as far as I know. I've neglected my family in the last couple of years. I'm sure they've changed since I last saw them."

"I imagine they're making a simnel cake, too," Maureen said.

Mrs. Hoag smiled. "Yes. They would be doing this and letting it age a wee bit before Easter Sunday. And they are going on with their normal lives."

Her hands stilled in the marzipan mixture, and she looked solemnly at Maureen. "A long time ago I learned that the only permanent thing in life is change. In my grief at losing my husband, I forgot that. You should learn this at an early age, Maureen. You can accept change, and that includes losing loved ones, and get on with the life that God has given you, or you can fight change and be unhappy."

Maureen looked inside herself for the truth before she spoke. "I am trying very hard to change and be happy. But today what makes me happy is going back to the old ways and making the Easter cake."

"I wasn't meaning that we have to give up things that remind us of our loved ones. All we have left of them are memories." Mrs. Hoag moved beside Maureen and hugged her. "You don't need me telling you what is the natural way of life. You're a smart lass, you are."

Maureen hugged the old woman and glanced across at Mark. He looked bemused, as if he didn't understand their conversation.

CHAPTER 9

The Birds

Maureen got caught up in the Easter preparations at home, went skating with Mark on the Saturday afternoon after Easter, and attended a temperance march with Mother, and another full week passed before she remembered standing by the third-floor windows and seeing the figure down by the creek. It came back to her as she and Mark headed toward Mrs. Hoag's for their afternoon work and she saw some boys walking by the creek.

"How could I have forgotten?" she asked herself out loud.

"What?" Mark asked.

She explained about her earlier sighting. They made a detour from their regular route on the street from school to the mansion, parked their bicycles, and walked on the high side of the creek as it meandered toward Mrs. Hoag's home. The boys had already moved on, so Maureen searched for the exact spot where she had seen the figure.

"Not here, because we can't see the roof yet. I was looking down and saw him with something red." She trudged up a slight rise where the creek bank became a short bluff. Looking upward, she kept going until she could see the corner windows of the third-floor ballroom, and she nearly stumbled over an iron stake stuck in the ground.

"Here's the spot!"

"I don't see anything red," Mark said.

"I don't either, but it's been almost three weeks. Something or someone could have taken it." She studied the trampled brown ankle-high grass that last summer had stood much taller. Underneath, the ground was showing signs of new green now that May was around the corner. "It could be buried under this old growth."

"We'll have to come back later and look," Mark said, "or Mrs. Hoag will wonder where we are."

"I guess you're right. But I did see something."

"We don't work tomorrow after school. We can come search then," Mark said, and Maureen agreed that was a good plan.

They hurried toward the street, where it was easier to walk, and turned up the drive to Mrs. Hoag's house.

Maureen gasped and stopped stone still. A dead bird lay in her path.

"Poor thing," she said. "I wonder what happened to it."

"I'll get a shovel and bury it," Mark said in a manly voice. "That's what my father did once when a bird died in our yard. Go on in the house, Maureen, and tell Mrs. Hoag. I'll see if there's a shovel in that shed."

Maureen nodded and took a few more steps when she saw another dead bird off to her right.

"Oh no. Oh no," she repeated when she saw two more. They looked around and found five more dead birds, including one on the wide front porch.

"What's happened?" Mark asked. "Mrs. Hoag doesn't have a cat."

"We're going to need two shovels," Maureen said. "I'll go tell

Mrs. Hoag; then we'll give them a proper burial."

Mark started around the house toward the shed in the back-yard while Maureen knocked on the door.

Mark screamed, and Maureen jumped off the porch and ran to his side. She screamed, too.

"I can't believe this!" Mark yelled.

The backyard was covered with dead birds! There must have been a hundred of them. "Maureen! Mark!" Mrs. Hoag called from the front porch.

Maureen rushed back to the porch. "They're all dead!" she shouted and grabbed Mrs. Hoag's hand and led her to where Mark stood.

"Oh my. Oh my." Mrs. Hoag had tears in her eyes. "Are they all dead?" she finally asked. "How could this happen?"

Maureen had no answer, and they stood looking for the longest time at the carnage in the backyard. It was eerie, seeing all those dead birds covering the ground. The bird feeders, like soldiers, stood guard over the birds.

"What could have caused this?" Mark asked.

"They got sick," Maureen said. It was the first thing that crossed her mind. That was what had happened to her mama. At first Mama had thought she had eaten something that had dis-agreed with her, but she got sicker and sicker, and within a few days she had died. "Or they ate something that disagreed with them."

Maureen looked up at the tall bird feeders. The upturned glass jars were half filled with seed, and more seed was scattered in the backyard. Had the seed been poisoned? Why would Mrs. Hoag poison birds when she loved them so much? *Because she is crazy,*

Maureen thought. Then she immediately felt ashamed. She had grown to love Mrs. Hoag, and she knew the woman wasn't crazy, no matter what the others at school said. Maybe Mrs. Hoag had been misunderstood these last two years, but she wasn't crazy.

"When did you fill these up?" Maureen asked Mrs. Hoag.

"It's been a week at least," she answered. "I put it out for the flocks that are just coming back north. There haven't been that many yet."

"When did you get the seed? Is it old? Could it have gone bad?"

Mrs. Hoag shook her head, her gaze still on the dead birds. "I went to the feed store the day after Easter. I remember it distinctly, because I also bought some arsenic for the mice that have gotten in the house. Bertha had said— Oh no! You don't think I put them together, do you?"

Maureen glanced at Mark, who looked like that was exactly what he thought.

"No. You wouldn't do that," Maureen said. "Where did you put the seed?"

"In the back room. I always keep it there so it will stay cool but dry."

"Show me," Maureen said. She took Mrs. Hoag by the hand again, and the threesome walked into the house through the back door.

"Right over here," Mrs. Hoag said and pointed to a feed sack. "I had the man at the feed store mix it for me."

"Where did you put the poison?" Mark asked.

"Bertha put it in the garden shed. I watched her sprinkle it behind cupboards so that Ruthie wouldn't get in the stuff, then

93

I had her put it in the shed."

The trio zigzagged out to the shed, carefully avoiding stepping on any of the dead birds, which were concentrated under the bird feeders. Mark opened the door and led the way inside.

The open bag of powder lay on the dirt floor, its contents scattered about it as if someone had dropped it.

"When she came out here with it, the bag was tied tight," Mrs. Hoag said. "Come, let's ask her."

Again they made their way carefully across the backyard and back into the house. Mrs. Hoag questioned Bertha, who said she put the bag on the back shelf of the shed as Mrs. Hoag had requested. That had been more than two weeks ago.

"Then someone else got the bag of poison and put arsenic in the bird feeders," Mark said.

"And it must have been done today or last night," Mrs. Hoag said. "That poison would have immediately killed the birds."

"What about the feeders in the front yard?" Maureen asked. "We didn't find many birds there."

They trooped to the front yard and discovered that the few feeders there still held great amounts of bird seed. The few dead birds weren't close to the bird feeders.

"The killer didn't put the poison in the front feeders," Mark said. "He only put it in the back ones. He was probably afraid of being seen."

Maureen nodded. That was exactly what she thought, too.

"Who did this?" Mrs. Hoag shouted. The anger fled from her voice and a mournful tone replaced it. "What do we do with all these poor dead birds?"

"I'll call Mother," Maureen answered.

Once again they went inside, and Mark and Mrs. Hoag sat on the couch while Maureen used the telephone in the Oriental Room.

"Quiet, be quiet." Ruthie waddled in. "Quiet."

"Mother will be right over," Maureen said. "Mrs. Hoag, have you taught Ruthie to say that?"

As if on cue, Ruthie said, "Quiet, be quiet."

"I've not been saying that," Mrs. Hoag said.

"I think someone who has come in here and stolen that Remington statue has said that, and Ruthie has heard him."

"Them," Mark said. "Remember, we thought there had to be two of them, and one of them said it to the other one."

Maureen remembered, but they had never mentioned it to Mrs. Hoag. The first day they heard Ruthie say that was the same day they had met the president, and the excitement of that day had pushed Ruthie's new phrase out of Maureen's mind.

"And what about the figure I saw by the creek and something red?" Maureen asked. "Maybe that person is the one who poisoned the birds."

"There are many strange things going on," Mrs. Hoag said. "And I'm not sure of what you're saying. What figure?"

Maureen explained about what she'd seen on the day Bertha had cut her hand in the kitchen.

"There are too many things to be remembering," Mrs. Hoag said. "Mark, get my paper and pen off the library desk."

He ran to do her bidding; then Mrs. Hoag took the items and wrote WHAT WE KNOW at the top of the page.

"Let's start at the beginning," she said.

"Your handbag was stolen," Mark said.

Mrs. Hoag wrote that down.

"The Remington was stolen. And other art in the Western Room was taken and replaced by other pieces," Maureen said. "Did the police say anything about them?"

"They took a description of the items and said to lock the doors. I don't know that they believed that something was taken, even though I showed them the photograph of *The Wicked Pony*."

"There was a footprint in the secret staircase," Mark said.

"What footprint?" Mrs. Hoag asked at the same moment that a knock sounded on the front door.

Maureen ran to the door. "Mother, I'm so glad you came." Maureen reached out and hugged her. She hadn't done that since the day Mama had died, but it seemed right, and Mother put her arms around Maureen. "Something frightful is happening here."

Mrs. Hoag explained about the birds, and once more they trudged to the backyard.

"This is horrible," Mother said with her hand to her mouth.

"What do we do?" Maureen asked.

Mother gazed at the birds, nodded her head as if she'd made up her mind, and took charge. "We must burn them. Dead animals can carry disease, so we must dispose of them immediately. Mrs. Hoag, do you have some shovels we can use, and where can we start a fire?"

They decided to burn them right in the backyard so they didn't have to move the birds far. Mark carried some hot coals out from the furnace and helped Mother start the fire. Mother called Greta and their odd-jobs man to come down and to bring shovels and also called Father at the bank and told him what had happened.

"We need some dry wood to keep the fire going," Mother said.

Maureen and Mark carried small twigs from beneath trees and then some small logs from the wood pile.

Soon they had a bonfire blazing. Greta and the odd-jobs man arrived by the time Mother threw the first bird on the fire. The stench of singed feathers filled the air as dead bird after dead bird was added to the small inferno.

Maureen felt her stomach churn from the sight of the burning corpses. Now that help had arrived, she turned her back on the fire and walked to the side yard to escape the smoke and the mayhem.

A roar from the street caused her to look toward the front yard, and she saw the German car that Father had admired pull into Mrs. Hoag's drive. Sidney Orr climbed out of the driver's seat and strode toward her.

"What's going on?" he asked. "Where's Lillian?"

"Mrs. Hoag's in the backyard," Maureen said. She was going to explain more, but he marched past her. Maureen followed him.

"Lillian," he said and held out his hands to embrace her. Mrs. Hoag held a shovel and didn't put it down to take his hands. "I was happening by and saw the fire. What's going on?"

Mrs. Hoag explained while the others periodically added more birds to the flames.

"You must leave here," he said. "Someone is playing a malicious prank on you. You're welcome to come stay with me and my wife."

"Thank you, Sidney, but I'm fine here. No one poisoned *me*."

"But you could be next," he said.

Maureen saw fear in Mrs. Hoag's eyes, but then it was quickly gone. "I'll be fine. We just need to be getting rid of these birds."

Mr. Orr took the shovel from her and threw some birds into the fire.

"Come with me, Mrs. Hoag," Maureen said. "Come away from the fire." She led the woman to the side yard, but Mrs. Hoag wouldn't turn her back to the flames.

"I don't like losing my bird friends," she said as she wiped a tear from her eye. "I like having them in the yard. I like watching them out the window. When Franklin first died, I started watching the birds come and go. That's when I put up the bird feeders. Bertha and I put them up ourselves. Now I best be taking them down and getting the poison out before other birds land here."

Maureen hadn't thought of that. There were grains all over the ground. Would they poison a whole new flock?

"We'll rake up these seeds," Maureen said with a catch in her voice, "and burn every one."

It took several hours before the fire died down and the last bird had been burned. Father and Uncle Albert had come after the bank closed, and they took over the fire and sent the women into the house. Maureen saw Sidney Orr leave soon after Father arrived.

"Should we call the police and tell them what happened?" Maureen asked.

"I don't know that it would do any good," Mrs. Hoag said. "When I reported the artwork stolen and replaced by other art, they looked at me very oddly. They said thieves don't replace things they've taken. Now I have a yard full of poisoned birds. What's happening, Maureen?" she asked in a sorrowful voice. "This is making me crazy."

CHAPTER 10

The Footprint

Even though it was late when they got home that night, Mother had insisted that Maureen wash her hair.

"We all smell like smoke," she said. "Let's get rid of any vestige of this evening's adventure that we can."

Both Mother and Maureen sat on the floor in front of the fireplace, finger-combing their long hair to dry it, when Maureen asked, "Why would someone poison those birds?"

"I've been thinking about that, too," Mother said, "and I can't find a reason."

"Mrs. Hoag said it was making her crazy. . .the things that have happened lately. Do you think someone is trying to make her crazy?" That was the only explanation Maureen could come up with, and it didn't make sense. She'd grown to love Mrs. Hoag, yet there was always a niggling doubt about her that kept creeping in from time to time.

"Mother, you said she was an important person to the community before her husband died, but now everybody thinks she's crazy. Mark called her Crazy Old Lady Hoag when we found her handbag. The girls at school think she's crazy. Why do people call her that?"

Mother pulled her long hair back from her face and looked at

99

Maureen. "People aren't always very kind. Maybe it's human nature, I don't know, but they seem to pick on one person who's a little different just to make themselves feel superior."

"Like the women at your meeting picked on Carrie Nation?" Maureen didn't say it out loud, but she thought of how the girls at school had picked on her. Maybe they hadn't exactly picked on her, but they had excluded her, and it felt like the same thing.

"Carrie Nation is destroying other people's property. We want our movement to be peaceful but forceful, and she is going against our principles. That's why the women are talking against her. She's raging against alcohol."

"Mrs. Hoag hasn't raged against anything."

"No, she hasn't. She withdrew into her home for a long time, shunning people, but she's not the first person to deal with grief that way. People have been unkind to her because she changed so much—from being out in public all the time to being a recluse. Now she's changing back to the way she was, and I believe you've helped her do that." Mother reached over and stroked Maureen's soft hair. "I have admired how you've dealt with your own grief, Maureen. Carleen's memory will always be with you, but you've kept on living. I know this must be so very difficult for someone your age."

Maureen felt tears sting her eyes at the mention of her mama. "I talk to her picture," she confessed. "Does that make me crazy?"

Mother pulled her into her arms. "That makes you very normal. I still talk to my mother in my mind. I do something good, and I wonder if it would make her proud of me. Or I do something bad, and I know she'd be displeased because that was not the way she taught me."

Maureen gasped. "You don't do anything bad."

Mother laughed. "I try not to, but I sometimes think unkind thoughts, and I want to do better than that. My mother taught me to live by the Golden Rule, and I believe that is the only way to live; but sometimes I slip."

Maureen shook her head. "That's not possible. You're the best person I know."

"And you're the best daughter in the world," Mother said as the grandfather clock in the hall struck eleven. "Oh, it's late. We're going to be tired tomorrow, but I wouldn't exchange this time together for two weeks of sleep." She kissed Maureen on the forehead and walked her to her bedroom, where they said their nightly prayer.

The next day the story of the bird kill spread through the school. Maureen had hoped that Mark wouldn't mention it to anyone because it would just give the girls another chance to talk badly about Mrs. Hoag, but he claimed he hadn't said a word before he heard others talking.

"Sidney Orr told my father," Sarah said during the noon break. "Mrs. Hoag probably poisoned them herself."

"She didn't!" Maureen exclaimed. "Someone is doing this to upset her, and I'm going to find out who."

"So now Maureen's a female policeman," Sarah said and laughed at her own joke. "A female policeman." The others around them on the school grounds joined in.

This was what Mother had been talking about. People picking on one person to make them feel like they were smarter and better. Well, Maureen would find out who was doing this to Mrs. Hoag. Somehow, she would find out. Then she'd show them. Problem was, school would be out at the end of the week, and she doubted that she'd discover who the bird killer was by then. She would see some of the girls during the summer at Sunday school. She'd make sure they found out about the bird killer once she found him.

She sat in history class that afternoon and completed a list of suspicious things that Mrs. Hoag had started the evening before. She showed it to Mark after school as they walked to the mansion. It wasn't their workday, but they both wanted to check on the old woman. And Mark had a plan.

"I think the person who took the statue is the same one who left a footprint in the staircase. We have to catch him, and I know how."

Maureen still wasn't convinced that the footprint wasn't mud off Mark's boot, but she listened as he explained about putting powder on the stairs and how then the thief would leave a trail.

"How do you know this?"

"I read it in a dime novel. Bowery Billy did it, and he caught the bad man," he explained as they climbed the front porch steps.

Mrs. Hoag wasn't home. Bertha said she'd gone downtown to the library.

"Can we come in and check on something?" Mark asked.

"I suppose that won't hurt," Bertha said and held the door wide. She left them in the Oriental Room.

"Stay on guard," Mark said. "Mrs. Hoag said Bertha didn't know about the secret staircase, so we can't let her find us there." He pushed on the secret panel and looked in the staircase. "No new footprints, but we haven't had rain. Now, we need some powder."

"I saw some talcum powder in the bathroom that day I got the bandages for Bertha's cuts," Maureen said.

"Good. Go get it," Mark said in a low voice.

"Yes, Bowery Billy," Maureen said with a soft chuckle. Still, she fell in with his plan, tiptoed to the bathroom, and returned with the talcum.

"It's got to be very light or the thief will see it," Mark said as he gently sprinkled powder over the bottom landing of the staircase. "If he comes in through the Oriental Room panel, he'll leave a footprint on the stair. If he comes down this way, he should leave a footprint on this rug."

As soon as he had finished and Maureen had returned the talcum powder to the bathroom, they wandered into the kitchen and told Bertha they were leaving.

"Tell Mrs. Hoag we'll be here tomorrow after school," Mark said.

The next day, they fairly flew to the mansion to check the staircase, although Maureen also wanted to search the creek bank for something red that the mysterious figure had left there. That would have to wait until Saturday, she concluded, but she wanted to add it to Mrs. Hoag's list of what they knew. She carried her own list of suspicious items in her skirt pocket.

Mrs. Hoag opened the door and ushered them in. "Bertha said you came by yesterday."

Mark explained about the powder and his theory that the thief used the secret staircase. "Can we check it?"

"Be my guest," she said.

Mark pushed the panel back, quickly lit the lantern, and held it over the landing so they could all see. The talcum powder was gone.

"There's nothing there," Mrs. Hoag said.

"He put a light dusting on there," Maureen said as Mark took the light and headed to the top of the stairs. "How could it be gone? You didn't sweep it up, did you?"

"I haven't opened the stairs at all," Mrs. Hoag said.

"I found one," Mark called down.

Maureen climbed as fast as she could, which wasn't very fast, since she didn't have the light and needed to feel her way along. When she reached Mark, he showed her a footprint of the toe of a boot. It was faint, but it was a footprint made of powder.

"Isn't that odd?" he said. "They wiped everything clean except for this print. Why?"

That was the same question that they had been asking for weeks. Why?

"Let's make sure nothing's missing," Mrs. Hoag said when they reported to her.

Again they went room by room with the cataloging list. And again they found a statue missing in the Western Room and replaced with another one. Nothing else was bothered.

"The thief likes Western art," Mrs. Hoag said. "Let's go back downstairs and talk."

They followed her downstairs, and this time Maureen saw that Mrs. Hoag had the tea service set out, like the time they had talked with her about taking the job. In her earlier rush to the stairs, Maureen hadn't noticed it.

Mrs. Hoag poured them each a cup of tea, then she sat back on the couch. "After we burned the birds Tuesday evening, I got scared. Bertha and I went to the West Hotel and spent the night, although I didn't get any more sleep than I would have if I'd stayed here. I sat in that hotel room and had a long talk with myself."

She stood and walked to the secret staircase panel and pushed it open, then closed it again. "Someone is trying to frighten me. I don't know who, but he's been a success. Franklin would be ashamed of my behavior. He would have wanted me to fight this person, and I'm going to," she said and clenched her fist.

"I am staying here. No one is going to scare me out of my home again. And I want to open my house as a children's museum. I want each room to appear as a room from another country instead of just a place to store our souvenirs and artwork. That would take a bit of work and maybe another trip or two, but it would be fun. I've been rotting in this house since Franklin died, and it's time I made peace with that and moved forward."

"Would you still live here?" Mark asked.

"Oh yes. This mansion is so large, I could live very well in one part and let the rest be the museum."

"That's wonderful," Maureen said as a knock sounded at the front door.

Mrs. Hoag answered it and ushered Sidney Orr into the room. He held a bouquet of roses, obviously from a flower shop, and after taking one out, he handed them to Mrs. Hoag.

"To cheer you up after that horrible ordeal with the dead birds," he said. "And this one is for your little friend." He walked over to Maureen and handed her the rose.

"Thank you," she said. "Nobody's ever given me a flower before."

Mr. Orr smiled down at her. Mrs. Hoag got a vase for her roses and brought in another teacup for Sidney.

"How are you doing, Lillian?"

Mrs. Hoag told him about the missing artwork, but she didn't mention the footprint on the secret staircase.

"Have you called the police?"

"They are aware of some stolen art in the past. I shall call them again."

"Lillian, I don't like this. If someone's getting into your house, you may be in danger. First the birds; you could be next. Have you thought about my offer? This is too big a house for one person."

"No, no," she answered. "I'm not leaving my home."

"It might do you some good to get away from this house," he said with a smile. "My offer to buy it still stands. You did say you'd give it serious thought."

"I have, and my home is not for sale. I was just telling my friends that I want to open a children's museum. Let youngsters come and see things exactly as they would be in the country they came from. It would seem children were getting to travel without leaving this city. It would be quite different from a regular museum, and I believe it would be successful."

Mr. Orr glanced at Maureen and Mark. "I can see you've made up your mind, Lillian. I'm sure your museum will be well received. But what about the rest of your land? Have you got anything planned for it?"

"Not right now, but I'm sure we'll be finding a use for it."

"If you change your mind, let me know." Sidney Orr rose to his feet. "I'll be checking to see that you're all right. Keep the doors locked."

"I'll do that, Sidney, but don't worry. I'll be fine." Mrs. Hoag led the way to the entry and opened the door for him, then returned to the Oriental Room.

"Mr. Orr thought you should leave," Maureen said. "I'm thinking that, too."

"I did, too, Tuesday night. But not now. It's my home, and I'm staying. Right now I'm going to drive to the police station and report the latest robbery. Talking face-to-face is better than using the telephone. I want to find out who's doing this."

"What about work?" Mark asked.

"We'll start again on Saturday. No, wait. Nadine told me tomorrow's the last day of school, and I'm thinking you should have some time to celebrate. Come over Monday morning, and we'll set up a new schedule for the summer."

Chapter 11

Citizenship!

School was out for the summer. To start the summer off right, Mother and Father took Maureen to the symphony on Saturday night. They included Mrs. Hoag in their plans, and the evening was a grand success.

No one mentioned the dead birds or the stolen art. Instead, the evening was a gala event with dress-up clothes and fabulous music.

Mrs. Hoag seemed grateful to be included. She squeezed Maureen's hand tightly as they walked into the symphony hall, and she was greeted from all sides. She must have known everyone in the lobby. At first, she wouldn't let go of Maureen's hand, but then she had to because women were coming up and hugging her and kissing her on the cheek.

Maureen heard, "Lillian, it's so good to see you here," over and over.

As they settled into their auditorium seats, Mrs. Hoag said, "This is the first time I've seen most of these people since Franklin's funeral. Thank you for making me come."

"I didn't make you come," Maureen said.

"You asked me, and I didn't know how to turn you down. Thank you, dear, for bringing me back into the life of the city."

The brand-new symphony enchanted Maureen, who'd never

heard anything like it. The music carried her along, and her heart soared with the emotion in the powerful sounds.

She tried to describe it to Mark the next morning after Sunday school but couldn't explain it well. "You'll have to come with us next time," she said.

"Father said he's going to take me so I can hear the great brass section," Mark said. "We would have gone last night, but the whole family went to our neighbor's seventieth birthday party, which was pretty dull."

"For excitement we could go to Mrs. Hoag's creek tomorrow morning before we learn our summer work schedule."

"Yes! We can search for the something red that the person dropped," Mark said.

They agreed on a time, and Mark rode his bicycle over early Monday morning. Maureen opened the door when he knocked.

"Come in. You won't believe the good news. Come in." She grabbed his arm and dragged him inside to the parlor where Mother was talking on the telephone.

"What in the world?" Mark asked.

"Shh. . ." Maureen held her finger to her lips and nodded toward Mother. She cocked her head to one side, listening to the one-sided conversation. Mother's eyes danced with excitement, and she nodded her head as if the lawyer on the other end could see it.

"At the judge's earliest convenience," she said. "Ten o'clock will be fine. Thank you for taking care of this."

She hung up the phone and grabbed Maureen. "Friday morning at ten. We'll have a luncheon afterward. Who would you like to invite? Who would you like to attend the ceremony?"

"What's going on?" Mark asked.

"I'm going to be a citizen," Maureen sang. "I'm going to be a citizen of the United States of America."

"That doesn't give us long to plan," Mother said, "but I figured we should take the earliest date." She had already reached for a pen and paper and was jotting down notes. "We'll have Mark's family, of course, and Mrs. Hoag. What about the girls at school?"

Maureen looked at Mark and shrugged.

"Ask all of them," he said.

"All of them?" Maureen echoed. Both the wealthy girls in Sarah's group and the daughters of servants who had pretty much ignored her since she'd been adopted? Well, why not? In her present mood, she was feeling very generous and forgiving. Why not ask all of them? The servants' daughters could see how easy it was to become a citizen, and the wealthy girls could meet Mrs. Hoag and see that she was a wonderful person.

Maureen named the girls as she pointed to her fingers, counting them off. "Have I forgotten anyone?" she asked Mark.

"What about Ross and Aaron and Dominic?"

Why shouldn't she invite Mark's friends? They had included her at school in games when the girls hadn't.

"How many can we have?" she asked.

"The main table will hold eighteen, but we can set up a smaller table in the dining room. We need to get out invitations today, and then there will be the menu to plan. Ice cream and cake for dessert?"

"Yes. Oh yes," Maureen said.

They talked awhile longer about the luncheon, then Mark reminded Maureen that they should get over to Mrs. Hoag's.

Maureen rode Mother's bicycle alongside Mark's up the drive to the front porch. The exploration of the creek area would have to wait until after they talked to Mrs. Hoag.

Once again, Mrs. Hoag had the tea service out, which Maureen knew meant they would have a discussion.

"This is a celebration," Mrs. Hoag said, once Maureen had told her the news about the swearing-in ceremony and the luncheon. "I'll call Nadine and see what I can do to help with the planning. Now, about your summer work hours." She went into detail about cataloging the rest of the house before they started planning each museum room.

"What will the Western Room be?" Mark asked.

"I may have to divide that into several rooms. I'm going to decorate a room to look like Theodore Roosevelt's ranch house in Dakota, with an Indian blanket on the back of the couch, just like I remember his main room."

"Will you keep all the statues?" Maureen asked.

"Yes, but we will only put one or two in the actual ranch room. The others will be displayed in a special art section. There are lots of details to work out. I'm going to create a board of directors, just like at the museum downtown. I want children as well as adults on it. And you two must be members. Do you accept board positions?" she asked solemnly.

"I do," Maureen said.

"Yes," Mark said.

"Well done. Then we should get to work in the Egypt Room today."

They worked until noon. After eating with Mother, Maureen and Mark left to deliver the luncheon invitation to the printer's. On their return trip, they detoured by the creek, pushing their bicycles onto Mrs. Hoag's grounds and leaving them near the street to explore the rest of the way on foot.

As they approached the area where Maureen had seen the figure, they heard whistling. Looking down the short bluff to the creek, Maureen saw a boy, a few years older than she, carrying a fishing pole and walking along the ledge that was about a foot above the water.

"What are you doing?" she called.

He looked startled and nearly dropped his fishing pole. "Nothing. Just looking around."

"You come here often?" Mark asked.

"Sometimes. There aren't any fish in here, though. None big enough to keep anyway."

"Oh," Maureen said and backed away from the edge of the bluff. She didn't want to look for something red with the boy around. "Let's go, Mark. Mother may need us to run other errands for her."

"Could he have been the person you saw?" Mark asked as soon as they were back on their bicycles.

"I don't know. It was hard to tell an age, but it could have been him."

It was late afternoon before they went back to the creek, and they only had a few minutes. Maureen located the spot by the old iron stake in the ground. Although they walked in ever-widening circles, they didn't see anything red.

The rest of that week, they didn't have time to search. Preparations for the luncheon took time. Mark helped with the decorations, even though he was reluctant to get involved at first.

"We couldn't add another flag anywhere," he said on Thursday afternoon when they stood back and admired their work in the dining room. Each place setting had a small flag, and the large table and the smaller one were covered with red tablecloths. Red, white, and blue bunting draped the buffet table.

On Friday morning, Father drove Maureen, Mother, and Mrs. Hoag to the courthouse. Uncle Albert and Aunt Annie, Mark, and his brother and sisters were already there when they arrived.

The group was ushered into the judge's chambers for the ceremony. Maureen had brought the Bible that Mother had given her when she'd joined the new church, and the judge held it while Maureen put her hand on it and swore allegiance to the United States and disavowed her citizenship in Ireland.

"Maybe someday you can go back to Ireland to see where you were born," Mrs. Hoag said after the judge had declared Maureen a citizen and she and Mother and Father had signed the official papers. "You don't want to lose sight of where you came from, but it's a better place for you here."

Congratulations came from everyone. Father had brought the Brownie camera and let Mark take snapshot after snapshot. Aunt Annie hugged Maureen, and Mark patted her on the back. When the excitement wore down, they walked back outside to a bright May morning to load up for the trip home for the luncheon.

Uncle Albert pulled Maureen aside. "This is a big day," he said. "We take for granted what you have become—a citizen of this great country." He reached in his pocket and pulled out a chain with a round disk charm dangling from it. An image of a teddy bear was engraved on the small pendant, and the words TEDDY ROOSEVELT were inscribed below. "This is to remind you that you've met the president of the United States. Not many citizens can claim that honor."

"Thank you, Uncle Albert," Maureen said and took the necklace. "I'll wear it always." She hooked it behind her neck and let it dangle in front.

"Smile," Mark called. He pointed the camera at them and clicked a picture of his father with Maureen.

Back home, both families and Mrs. Hoag assembled on the front porch for more pictures.

"Stay here," Father instructed Maureen. He went inside and returned a moment later wheeling a brand-new girl's bicycle. "Every new citizen should have a way to get around," he said. "Now you don't have to ride Mother's bicycle, and the three of us can go on rides together."

"If we can get him away from the automobile," Mother said, and the rest laughed.

"We can ride everywhere," Mark said.

And they could. Mother's bicycle was too large, and Maureen had ridden it standing up instead of sitting on the seat.

"Thank you," Maureen said and hugged her mother and father.

She didn't have a chance to ride it then, since the luncheon guests were expected right at noon, and they needed to make certain all was done before Maureen's classmates arrived.

At a quarter to twelve, the first of the girls knocked on the door. A couple more trickled in a few minutes later, and Mark's friends arrived; but it was the stroke of noon before Sarah and her group of friends came all together. Maureen had feared they wouldn't come.

"We didn't want to miss a party," Sarah said to Mark, but Maureen overheard her. "We heard you were having ice cream."

Maureen had thought her citizenship would help Sarah see her in a different light, but it would obviously take a lot more than that. Maureen made sure that the wealthy group were seated among the poorer girls. Sarah picked up her place card from the small table and attempted to move it.

"I should sit at the main table," Sarah said and took another girl's place card from the big table to trade with hers.

"You should sit where your place card was," Mark said and took the place card away from Sarah and put it back the way Maureen had it.

Sarah glared at him and Maureen, but she took her assigned seat.

As soon as they were all seated, Father clinked a spoon against his glass and asked for quiet. He offered a prayer of thanksgiving that Maureen had come to this country and that she was now a citizen. And he asked for God's blessing on her life.

"Amen," Uncle Albert said in a strong voice when the prayer ended.

Father asked Maureen to introduce each person so they would all know one another. Maureen stood and swallowed hard, then started naming the guests. She decided being a member of the Stevenson family meant speaking in front of others a lot, and she'd better get used to it. She noticed many curious stares from the girls when she introduced Mrs. Hoag, and she was glad the older woman looked quite handsome in a fashionable green dress.

The guests moved quietly down the buffet line, then chatter took over as they again took their seats at the tables.

"It was a good party," Mother said later after the last of the guests had departed. "I noticed that Sarah Noble resented being at the smaller table."

"Mother, I have not lived by the Golden Rule," Maureen confessed.

"Let me guess. You put Sarah at the small table because you knew she wouldn't like it."

"Yes," Maureen admitted.

"Several people had to sit at the small table. And probably all those who sat there would have preferred being a part of the larger group." She put her arm around Maureen. "If you were seated at a smaller table at a party like this, would you have acted as rudely as Sarah did?"

"No," Maureen said honestly.

"Well, then, I think this is one of those instances where you must learn that you will not always be liked by everyone. And although we should try to be friends and treat others in a kind manner, others may not always treat us kindly back. Don't let it worry you, Maureen. Remember to turn the other cheek, smile, and go on."

At Sunday school some of the other girls made a point of talking to Maureen. Sarah did not; but this time it didn't bother Maureen. She followed Mother's advice and smiled.

Monday morning found Mark and Maureen back at Mrs. Hoag's, this time in the Hawaiian Room.

"I think we will lower the ceiling in here over part of this room and use a thatched roof for the house," Mrs. Hoag said. "We'll make the rest of this room look as if it's outdoors with the sandy beaches and sprinkle it with some of these shells. I've never seen the ocean as blue as it was in Hawaii."

"Could we paint that wall over there blue?" Mark said. "Then it would look like water."

"I'm glad you're a board member for the museum," Mrs. Hoag said. "You have good ideas."

Bertha appeared at the door of the Hawaiian Room and said Mrs. Hoag was wanted on the telephone. Mrs. Hoag disappeared downstairs and returned a moment later with a stony look on her face.

"Mark, your mother needs you at home."

"Right now?" he asked.

"Yes, right now. Be gone with you. Maureen and I will work awhile longer."

Mark looked puzzled, but he quickly left.

Mrs. Hoag stood watching out the window. "He's on the street now. That's all the work we'll be doing for a while, Maureen."

"But you said we'd—"

"I know what I was saying, but that was so I wouldn't break down in front of Mark. He needs to be told by his mother."

"What's wrong?" Maureen asked with a tremble in her voice and foreboding in her mind.

"Your uncle Albert collapsed at the bank. They think it was his heart that stopped."

"He's. . .dead?" Maureen grasped the teddy bear charm on her necklace and knew the kindly man who had given it to her was gone.

CHAPTER 12

Mark's Sorrow

Maureen stood in stunned disbelief at the kitchen counter. She stirred vanilla cream pie ingredients as Mrs. Hoag and Bertha rolled out crusts.

"As soon as these pies are ready, we'll take them over to Mark's," Mrs. Hoag said. "That will give the family time to recover from the first shock. Nadine said church members are taking in food already."

Mother had called from Mark's house. She had gone there as soon as Father had called her and told her of Uncle Albert's death. How could a body up and die so suddenly? Mama had been sick for a few days. Not that Maureen had been prepared for her death, but she'd seen it coming at the end, when her mama got worse and worse.

Once again she grasped the teddy bear pendant. Never again would she see Uncle Albert's joyful smile or hear him say he wanted to shake the hand that shook the hand of the president.

How is Mark feeling now? She didn't want to go there, to that dark place she remembered of the first few hours after her mother's death. A heavy weight had descended on her chest, suffocating her, making it hard to breathe. *Poor Mark. He must be feeling that pain.*

"We must help him through this," Mrs. Hoag was saying. "We

must help him through this, although how he handles it will be up to him."

"He'll have pictures," Maureen said, remembering the pictures Mark had taken Friday when she'd become a citizen. At the house, Father had taken a group photograph of Mark's family. "I don't have pictures of my papa, but I talk to my mama's picture."

Mrs. Hoag nodded as if she understood, and they fell into silence as they finished making the pies. When they were baked and cooled, Maureen loaded them in the electric, and Mrs. Hoag drove to Mark's house.

Maureen recognized several of the buggies and wagons parked outside the Bowman home. The parson was there, and so was Father. His automobile was parked right in front.

With reluctant steps, Maureen walked behind Mrs. Hoag and carried two pies. They were met at the door by a woman from church.

"Just bring those pies right through here," she said and waved toward the back of the house. Maureen knew the way to the kitchen and left her pies on the table.

She had hoped to make it out of the house before she saw Mark, but he must have seen them come in, for he stood in the hall, blocking her escape.

"I'm so sorry," she said and burst into tears. Her chest heaved with heavy sobs. Mrs. Hoag put her arm around her and another around Mark and shepherded them to the front parlor where the family sat with friends.

Father left Aunt Annie's side and hugged Maureen.

"He gave me this," Maureen said between sobs and held out the teddy bear pendant. "Because I'm a citizen."

"I know," Father said. "He told me about it when he bought it. He loved you, Maureen. And he knew you loved him."

"I never told him." And, oh, how she wished she had.

"You don't have to explain love," Father said. "It's something people just know."

Maureen gulped and got the hiccups. She sneaked a glance at Mark and saw that his eyes were dry. She remembered the hour after her mama's death, when she'd cried her heart out, and then there were no more tears; but she also knew that the tears would come back.

"Let's get you a drink," Father said and took Maureen back to the kitchen. She drank a whole glass of water and then another one until her hiccups were gone. "Now, why don't you take Mark and Sophie outside?" he suggested. "They don't need to listen to their father's funeral plans."

Maureen took a deep breath, then did as Father asked. She and Mark and Sophie sat on the back porch steps. They sat in silence for a long time.

"He just fell down," Mark finally said. "They said he was dead before he hit the floor."

"Then he didn't hurt his head," Sophie said. "I hope he didn't hurt his head."

Sophie was only seven, and her focus on her father's pain touched Maureen. "I'm sure he didn't hurt his head," she reassured Sophie.

"He's in heaven, you know," Sophie said.

"I know. He's there with my mama and papa."

Mark looked at Maureen as if he finally understood what she'd gone through. His eyes looked hollow and older than when she'd seen him a couple hours earlier.

Odd how death made a person grow up. She wished she could go back to last summer, when she was more carefree; and she wished Mark could go back to yesterday, when they'd talked after Sunday school.

She wanted to help them, but she didn't know how. They sat there in the May sunshine, listening to the chatter in the kitchen. Mother came out once and sat down with them for a bit.

"The funeral will be Wednesday afternoon," she told them.

"Could we go for a walk?" Maureen asked. She remembered how activity had helped her pass the time after Mama's death.

"That's a good idea," Mother said. "I know you're not hungry, but come in and get something to eat first; then the three of you can get away from here for a while."

After they'd each grabbed a fried chicken leg and drunk a glass of milk, Mark led the way out of the house through the back door. Maureen knew she wasn't the only one who didn't want to see a lot of people.

They walked with no particular destination, but just walking helped Maureen feel better. It helped her headache, and it helped her heartache.

For a long time they walked in silence, past house after house, past vacant lots, and past their church and the cemetery.

"I guess we'll be here Wednesday," Mark said.

"Yes. If you think of something else, it helps," Maureen said. That's what she'd done. She'd concentrated on other things. On school, on a book she'd read. She'd struggled to block out her mama's funeral. And it had helped her get through it when all eyes were on her as she walked behind her mama's casket. Later she'd fallen apart again, but she had gotten through the ceremony. "I prayed over and over not to cry at the funeral, and I didn't," she said. "But I had to think of other things."

They turned around at the cemetery and walked back a different direction, past more houses where children played outside, laughing, obviously unaware of the heartbroken three who walked by.

They kept moving and changed directions, walking out toward a new section of town. Several houses were being built down one street. Carpenters' hammers pounded and workmen shouted. Maureen watched the activity as men unloaded lumber from a wagon.

"Look!" Mark exclaimed.

Maureen looked but saw nothing unusual. "What should I be seeing?"

Mark ran to the edge of the street and pointed to an iron stake with a scrap of red cloth tied to it.

"Something red," he said. He marched up to a workman and asked him something Maureen couldn't hear, then he ran back into the street where Sophie and Maureen waited.

"This marks the boundary of the yard for this house. Survey stakes. This must be what you saw in the woods by Mrs. Hoag's house."

"But why would there be survey stakes on Mrs. Hoag's land?"

"To build a house," Sophie said, "like this." She pointed to the house under construction.

"That's it. Someone wants to build houses on her land," Mark said. "And who do we know who wants to buy her land?"

"No," Maureen said, realizing what Mark was thinking. "Sidney Orr is a nice man. He gave me a flower."

"He wants to buy Mrs. Hoag's house. We heard him say so. And he asked about her property."

"But why would he have the land divided up for houses before he bought the land?"

"Maybe he needed to know how many houses he could build there so he could get a loan from the bank. I'll ask Father," Mark said. Then, as if realizing what he had said, he put his hand over his mouth. He closed his eyes, but tears oozed out.

"You have to cry sometime," Maureen said. "Let's go back to your house."

It was as if a dam had burst and let Mark's emotions out. He talked about his father and all the things they had done together.

"He took me to a Millers baseball game last summer," Mark said. "He said we'd go again this year."

They were some distance from the Bowman house, and they talked nonstop about Uncle Albert. Maureen remembered all the nice things he had done for her and how he had the greatest smile. Sophie talked about him reading to her at bedtime.

"He didn't like tinkering with things and fixing them like Uncle Theodore," Mark said. "He likes. . .liked," he corrected himself, "talking to people and making them feel better. And he liked knowing about places, new places."

"He told me he'd like to see Ireland," Maureen said. "He was a good Christian man. That's what Mrs. Hoag called him."

"I hope he didn't hurt his head," Sophie said again as they circled the Bowman house and walked up the back steps to the kitchen door.

The funeral on Wednesday afternoon was a good one as far as funerals went, Mother said later. Maureen had sat with Mark and

Sophie because Mother said it might help them.

The minister talked about what a good man Uncle Albert was, and then Father talked about him, and another man from the church also talked about how kind Uncle Albert was.

Maureen could hardly stand to look at Aunt Annie. At the cemetery she acted so strange, so quiet, and looked so lonely, even with her five children around her.

After the burial, the family went to the Bowman home for a big dinner served by the church women. The mood was more lighthearted then, as if everyone had given a huge sigh of relief, but Maureen knew that it was temporary. It had been only five months ago that she'd felt that same relief after Mama's funeral. She knew the pain would come back, and she felt old beyond her years for knowing it.

"The best thing to do for them is to listen to them talk about Albert and keep them busy building a different life," Mother said when she and Maureen and Father had returned home.

"Mrs. Hoag said we didn't need to work until Mark felt up to it," Maureen said.

"I don't think that's a good idea," Mother said. "She told me he might need time alone, but that's what she did and it got too easy for her to stay away from other people. Why don't you call Mark tomorrow and see if he's willing to work a little bit? Just an hour, maybe, to get him out of the house a while."

Maureen telephoned Mark first thing the next morning, and he agreed to ride over to her house. "We could look down at the creek again," Maureen said, "then catalog some more."

They parked their bicycles at Mrs. Hoag's house, then cut across the land to the stake they had discovered earlier.

124

"It's got to be a survey stake," Mark said. "But why would it be right here by the edge of the creek?"

Maureen peered over the short bluff where they'd seen the boy fishing. "Maybe it marks something else. How did that boy get down there?" This was the only area around the creek that didn't have a flat bank to it.

The drop down the stone bluff to the foot-wide ledge that bordered the water was about six feet. Notches in the rock wall formed a natural ladder.

Mark climbed down first, then Maureen gathered her skirt about her and followed him. There were dried footprints along the ledge that ran about ten feet, then turned inward.

If she hadn't been looking for something, Maureen would have missed the opening. A rock wall jutted out and concealed the entry from the direction they were walking. The hole on the other side was small, but Mark and Maureen slid through it easily. A man could, too, but it would have been more of a squeeze.

"It's a cave," Maureen said. It couldn't have been more than four feet wide, but she couldn't tell how far back it went.

"I can't see a thing," Mark said.

"Me, either," Maureen agreed. "We ought to come back here when we have a light."

"You stay on that side, and I'll stay on this side, and we'll feel our way to the back," Mark said.

"For a little ways," Maureen said and hoped she didn't sound as scared as she felt. The place was cold and eerie. "If it goes too far back, we'll have to come back with a light. What are we looking for?"

"I don't know. But maybe that boy had been in this cave."

Maureen felt her way about six feet when the wall turned to

form the back wall, except it wasn't a stone wall. "There's wood back here," she said.

"Where?" Mark was a lot closer than she'd thought.

"Feel over here. The back wall is made of wood."

"What's this?" he asked, and Maureen heard a clink as he turned something over. "I think it's a lantern," he said. "There's a shelf here. Oh, wooden matches." He struck one, and the light nearly blinded Maureen, who was used to the darkness.

Mark lit the lantern then held it high. The back wall wasn't a wall at all but was a wooden door. It opened on well-oiled hinges.

"It's a tunnel," he said as the light exposed stone walls. There were timber beams overhead, and after the first twenty feet, the walls changed to mostly dirt.

Maureen had seen enough, but Mark kept going, and since he had the light, she followed. She turned her back once, and it was so dark, she couldn't see her hand. There was no noise underground. The smell of wet dirt filled her head. She felt alone, even though Mark walked just ahead of her with the lantern.

"I didn't cry at the funeral," Mark said suddenly.

The sudden mention of Uncle Albert shouldn't have surprised Maureen, but it did. Thoughts of Mama still crossed her mind at the oddest times.

"I know."

"Do you think Father's watching us in this cave?"

"I don't know. We can go back."

"No. I think he'd want us to explore it. He'd like knowing where it went. One time we went on a little lane outside of town just to see how far it would go." All the time he was talking, Mark walked forward. Within a couple more minutes, they reached the end of the tunnel and a ladder. Mark held the lantern up, and the light revealed a trapdoor overhead.

"What do we do now?" Maureen asked.

"We can't go back without finding out what's up there," Mark said.

"Do you hear anything?"

They were quiet a few moments and didn't hear a word. Then Maureen heard a voice. She held her breath until she heard it again.

"Quiet, be quiet."

"It's Ruthie," Mark exclaimed. "This must be the way the thieves get into the house to steal the artwork."

He handed Maureen the light and climbed up while she held the lantern. He had a little trouble pushing on the trapdoor. It wasn't hinged, so it didn't swing up easily. He applied so much pressure that it flew up a couple of inches and landed cockeyed off the hole with a loud thump. He pushed it to the side.

Stairs led higher, so he climbed up a couple steps to make room for Maureen. As soon as she was on the landing, she pushed the trapdoor back in place with her foot. This was familiar territory. She had been in the secret staircase a number of times. She handed the lantern back to Mark and pushed on the secret panel. It swung open, and she stepped out into the Oriental Room.

She saw Mrs. Hoag standing with the fireplace poker a fraction of a second before the woman hit her. Then all went black.

CHAPTER 13

The Plan

The next thing Maureen knew, she was on the couch with a wet cloth on her forehead. In a haze, she made out Mrs. Hoag leaning over her and Mark right beside her.

"Maureen, I'm so sorry. So sorry," Mrs. Hoag said over and over.

"She's coming to," Mark said as Maureen blinked her eyes again. "Are you all right?"

Maureen tried to talk, but it took too much effort, and nodding her head was worse. Keeping her eyes open was the best she could do.

"Maureen, I really tried not to hit you," Mrs. Hoag said. "The moment I saw it was you, I tried to stop swinging, but I'd started, and I couldn't stop it. Oh, I'm putting this badly."

"I'm all right," Maureen said. "I just need to be still a while." She touched the back of her head and felt a knot the size of a goose egg.

"I'll call Nadine," Mrs. Hoag said.

"No, I'm all right," Maureen said. She knew Mother had gone over to Aunt Annie's, and there was no need to upset her.

While Maureen recovered, Mark told Mrs. Hoag about the tunnel.

"I didn't know it existed," Mrs. Hoag said. "I wonder why

Franklin didn't tell me about it. Maybe he didn't know."

That didn't seem very likely to Maureen. If she'd lived in this wonderful old house, she'd have explored every inch of it and known all the secret closets and stairs and tunnels. She figured Franklin had played in that tunnel when he was young.

"We need to go back and hang up that lantern," Maureen said. "The thieves might come back and find out we know about the tunnel."

"They might already know," Mrs. Hoag said, "because of the time you used the powder. When they raised that trapdoor, all the talcum powder you put on it slid to the edge, and in that big amount, they would have noticed it and wiped it up. They must have missed that one footprint on the step."

"We still ought to put the lantern back," Mark said. "They know we knew about the staircase, but we didn't know then about the tunnel."

"You may be right," Mrs. Hoag said. "We'll see what the police say about it this time. Maybe now they won't think I'm imagining things."

She telephoned the police station, and an hour later a policeman knocked on the door. He was not the one Mrs. Hoag had talked to before, so she had to tell him the whole story from the beginning.

"I'd like to see the tunnel," the policeman said.

"We'll show you," Mark said. Maureen watched him pry up the trapdoor. Now that they knew it was there, Maureen could see a vague outline of it. But if a person wasn't looking, it was nearly invisible.

Maureen's head felt better and she didn't want to miss out on the excitement, so she got the lantern from the top of the stairs and followed Mark, the policeman, and Mrs. Hoag back through the tunnel to the creek bluff. It seemed like a shorter walk now that they knew where it led.

They inched their way along the narrow ledge by the water, and the policeman helped Mrs. Hoag climb up using the natural footholds. They carried the extra lantern and walked back to the house on Mrs. Hoag's land.

Once they were back inside the mansion, Mrs. Hoag got the "What We Know" list and showed it to the policeman. He took it with him when he left and said he would call about getting a policeman to stay there for the night so they could catch the thieves.

Cataloging seemed dull work after the excitement, so they only worked an hour before quitting. Mrs. Hoag thought Mark had worked long enough.

"It's hard to go home," Mark said as they went downstairs. "Mother is so sad."

"Let's have a cup of tea before you leave," Mrs. Hoag suggested. She had Bertha bring the tea service to the Oriental Room.

"Mark," she began once they were all served, "your father was a good man, and it will take your mother a long time to get over his passing. It took me two years of being alone before I was ready to move on in life. Your mother can't take that long because she has you children to guide and care for. But it will take her a while to lose the dullness in her eyes."

"I don't like being alone," Mark said with tears in his eyes. "It makes me think too much. I prayed that God would make me stop thinking about Father, but it didn't help."

"I did that, too," Maureen said. "I wondered. . .if God answers all prayers, why didn't He make the sadness go away? Mother said that God wants us to remember our loved ones. That His answer to my prayer was to give me time to grieve and to see that death is the natural way of things."

"Your mother's very wise," Mrs. Hoag said. "God gives us the gift of time. And He makes us think so we can remember. I still recall Franklin's laugh."

"Uncle Albert was very kind," Maureen said. "And thoughtful." She fingered her teddy bear pendant as she spoke.

"He read a lot of books," Mark said. "And he smiled a lot. He was a brave man, Mother said last night, because he always stood up for what was right."

"Your family talked about him last night?" Mrs. Hoag asked.

"Mother said the more we talk about Father, the more he will stay with us and the hurt will go away."

"Your mother's very wise, too," Mrs. Hoag said. They talked more about memories and how important they were.

"You want to eat at my house?" Maureen asked Mark when they had finished their tea. "Father will soon be home."

He nodded, and they rode their bicycles to Maureen's home. When Father came home for the noon meal, they told him about the tunnel.

"We didn't tell the policeman about the survey stake," Mark said.

"I thought about telling Mrs. Hoag," Maureen said, "but should we cast a bad light on Sidney Orr when we don't know for sure?"

"What's this about Sidney Orr?" Father asked.

Mark explained, and Father promised he would check through Uncle Albert's appointment book to see if Mr. Orr had talked to him about a loan to build houses.

"Of course, there are many other banks that would lend him money, but I'll see what I can find out about him. And, Mark, I know I can never take the place of your father, but if you ever want to talk about anything, please know you can come to me." Father ruffled Mark's hair as he spoke.

"Thank you, Uncle Theodore," Mark said. "I'll remember."

On Friday morning, Maureen and Mark hoped the police would have some news, but Mrs. Hoag said there had been no break-in. A policeman had stayed all night in the French Room, but there had been no sound from the secret staircase.

"Was there a certain day that we had break-ins?" Mrs. Hoag asked while they worked in the Mexico Room. "The police are going to stay one more night, but they asked if there was a certain night when the robberies occurred."

"It was on Thursday after the birds were killed that we saw the powder footprint," Mark said. "I don't remember the other footprint, but it had rained before then."

"The robbers could have taken the Remington any time before we noticed it was gone," Maureen said.

"So there's no real pattern," Mrs. Hoag said. "That's what I was thinking."

On Saturday, Mark rode his bicycle over to Maureen's before going to the cemetery, and they stopped by Mrs. Hoag's to see if there had been a break-in. Again, no one had climbed the secret stairs. The police had told Mrs. Hoag that they couldn't spare a man that evening but would try to continue the stakeout the next week.

"I think it will be tonight," Mark said as he and Maureen rode their bicycles to the cemetery to put lilacs on his father's grave.

"I wish we could stay there. My father would have said we should stay with Mrs. Hoag."

"Uncle Albert would have said that?" Maureen asked.

"He was the bravest man alive," Mark said. "Mother said he always stood up for what was right, and helping Mrs. Hoag is right."

Maureen agreed. "But we can't stay there. Mother won't let us."

"Maybe Uncle Theodore will. He said I could talk to him."

They put the lilacs on the grave, and Mark stepped back. "Father liked us helping Mrs. Hoag. He said she needed us, and she needs us tonight. I won't let Father down. He would have done this, and we will."

Maureen was not as convinced that Uncle Albert would have allowed them to stay at Mrs. Hoag's, but she didn't say so. Instead, she rode her bicycle downtown to the bank with Mark, where Father was busy on Saturday morning.

They waited a few minutes before they got to see him, but as soon as they were in Father's office, Mark said, "You told me I could talk to you." He explained about them staying at the mansion waiting for the robbers.

"Don't you think this is a job for the police?" Father asked.

"They won't stay tonight, so could we?"

"I'll have to speak to your mother," Father said. Maureen couldn't see Aunt Annie being agreeable to the plan, but she didn't say so, and she was surprised when Father hung up the phone and said the plan was on. "But I'm staying, too, and you have to agree to my rules. By the way, I checked Albert's appointment book, but there was no listing for Sidney Orr. You may be off base on that being a survey stake for housing. It may just be a marker for the robbers, since it was above the tunnel."

Maureen was glad to hear that. Since Mr. Orr had given her the rose, she'd had a special place for him in her heart. She had put the rose in a vase in her room for a while. Then she had pressed it in a book so she could keep it always. She also didn't want to tell Mrs. Hoag that her friend would do something dishonorable.

She didn't mention Sidney Orr when they stopped back by Mrs. Hoag's to tell her about the plan.

"Theodore called me," she said. "I think tonight will be the night they'll come, too."

Father's rules were very simple. Maureen and Mark could stay in the Western Room with him, but if there was the slightest sound from the French Room and the secret staircase, they were to slip safely into the little hidden closet and stay there. Father would signal Mrs. Hoag to call the police, who were on alert to come right over to the house and to the tunnel.

By eight o'clock, the plan was in place. Father sat by the door into the Western Room so he could quickly move downstairs. Maureen and Mark were behind tables nearby.

"Do you think they'll come before midnight?" Mark asked.

"No. Robbers would come in the dead of night, wouldn't they?" Maureen asked.

They heard the downstairs clock strike ten, eleven, and twelve. After that Maureen nodded off and didn't awake until six hours later. Early morning sunlight poured in the east windows.

"They didn't come?" she asked, disappointed.

"Not a sound," Father said. "I'm sure I would have awakened if they had come in. And no footprints." Mark had convinced them to put a light dusting of powder beside the secret panel in the French Room that led to the staircase in the wall.

"Maybe they will come tonight," Mark said with a yawn.

"Now wait a minute, Mark," Father said. "I agreed to one night."

"But the police won't stay again until Monday. We have to catch these thieves. They might harm Mrs. Hoag."

"I don't think she's in danger of that since they've had plenty of opportunity," Father said. "But I'll think about it."

They went to Maureen's house for breakfast, then they got dressed for Sunday school and church.

"Don't tell anyone what we did," Maureen warned Mark as they loaded into the automobile for the ride to church. "And let me talk to your mother."

It was the first time church had been held since Uncle Albert had died, and the minister remembered Aunt Annie and her family in the opening prayer and the closing one as well. Maureen could tell that Mark was feeling very sad when the service was over. He avoided looking her in the eyes and made his way quickly outside.

Aunt Annie's family was eating Sunday dinner at the Stevensons', so it was there that Maureen cornered her and asked about that night's repeat plan.

"Mark thinks Uncle Albert would have wanted him to help Mrs. Hoag," she said.

"Albert did think you and Mark had done a Christian service to Mrs. Hoag to bring her out of mourning," Aunt Annie said. "If Theodore will stay again, I have no objections."

Maureen told Mark, and together they talked to Father, who reluctantly agreed that they would try the plan again.

That night, they took their same positions. Just as the night before, Maureen heard the clock strike ten and eleven. Then she must have dozed. She awoke with a start when she felt a hand over her mouth. In the dim moonlight, she saw Mark right beside her. It was his hand. She nodded to let him know he could let go of her and she wouldn't speak.

She glanced around the table toward the Western Room door and saw Father standing beside it. He was motioning for them to get in the hidden closet as he tiptoed toward the big staircase to reach the telephone.

Maureen heard muffled footsteps coming from the French Room. She rose as quietly as she could and, with Mark, made her way to the closet. They had left the panel ajar so the sound of the spring-loaded door opening wouldn't alert the robbers. As they scrunched down inside, they left it open a sliver so they could see.

Father had disappeared down the stairs when the thieves stepped into the Western Room. From her vantage point, Maureen saw two figures walk cautiously into the room. One held a lantern, and the other held another statue.

"This is heavy. Why couldn't we take one of those vases downstairs?" one man said in a low voice.

"This is the last one we exchange up here. Next week we'll get lighter stuff," the other man said. "Maybe we can get several things in one trip."

"Quiet, be quiet." Maureen recognized Ruthie's voice as she waddled into the Western Room.

"What!"

"It's that parrot again. Hurry up, let's get out of here. That bird might wake up the old lady."

The men exchanged the statues and headed back to the French Room.

"They're getting away," Mark whispered. "Uncle Theodore hasn't had time to get downstairs yet." He pushed the secret panel open.

"Mark," Maureen hissed, "get back here." But he rushed out before she could stop him, so she bolted after him.

"What?" one of the men yelled.

"Quiet, be quiet," Ruthie squawked.

"We've got company!" the other man yelled.

Mark had reached the one carrying the statue, and he jumped on his back. Thrown off balance and unable to defend himself because he was holding the statue, the man tumbled to the floor.

"Get him off me!" he yelled at the other thief.

For an instant, Maureen stood frozen in fear, then she tackled the second thief. She was no match for him, and he threw her across the room as if she were a rag doll. He pulled Mark off the other man and grabbed the statue.

"Run!" he shouted, taking off for the French Room.

The man on the floor scrambled to his feet as Mark jumped him again. He shook Mark off and dashed to the secret stairs.

"Mark?" Maureen rushed to where he lay on the floor.

"I'm all right," he mumbled. "They got away."

Father ran into the room. "Are you all right? I told you to stay in the hidden room. I should never have left you up here." He hugged them both.

Mrs. Hoag scurried into the Western Room.

"They got away," Mark repeated. "But at least they're in the dark." He motioned to the lantern that the thieves had left behind.

CHAPTER 14

A Gift to America

"The police are on their way," Father said. "They know to go to the creek. All we can do is wait."

Maureen scurried over to the windows and looked out toward the creek. Mark, Father, and Mrs. Hoag followed and crowded against the windows. Even though the moon was half full, Maureen couldn't make out anything for a minute or so.

Then from the street she saw two horses and riders heading toward the creek bluff. The police had arrived.

Once the men rode to the creek, Maureen's sight was blocked by tree limbs now laden with new leaves.

"The police will get them now," Mark said. "I wonder who they are."

Maureen and Mark stared into the night for long minutes until they saw the policemen come back into sight. This time they were afoot with two other men.

"Thank the Lord they got them," Mrs. Hoag said as they filed downstairs. "Maybe I can have a whole night's rest now."

A policeman came to the door and reported that the thieves were being taken to jail. "We'll let you know tomorrow what we find out," he promised.

"It's time we went on home," Father said. "My bed will feel

mighty comfortable now. Mark, you can stay at our house for the rest of the night."

Maureen didn't think she'd be able to sleep, but fatigue overcame her and she actually slept until almost eight o'clock the next morning. She quickly dressed and hurried downstairs to the kitchen, where she found Mark eating a bowl of oatmeal.

"I can't believe I slept so long," she said. "Let's go to Mrs. Hoag's."

"First some breakfast, Maureen," her mother said. "I doubt that the police will call Mrs. Hoag until later this morning."

Maureen ate her oatmeal in big gulps, while Mark called his mother and told her about the night's excitement. As soon as Mother would let them, Maureen and Mark rode down to Mrs. Hoag's mansion.

"Any news?" Mark asked when Mrs. Hoag let them inside.

"Not a word, but I'll call them if they don't call this morning," she said. "Meanwhile, should we get back to work on the Mexico Room to pass the time?"

They discussed the events of the night in detail as they sat in the Mexico Room looking at various musical instruments and big sombreros. There were some sculptures mixed in, but the room didn't have any paintings.

"We should finish this today," Mrs. Hoag said.

But they didn't.

A policeman arrived and thoughts of cataloging fled from their minds.

They took their usual seats in the Oriental Room while the policeman told the story of the break-ins.

"One of the men, Jack Mercer, talked long and loud. He and his partner, Al Beechman, were hired to steal valuable art pieces from the house and replace them with lesser works."

"But why replace them? And who hired them?"

"They were hired by Sidney Orr," the policeman said.

Mrs. Hoag gasped. "Surely you're mistaken."

"No. We arrested him this morning. He had the Remington bronze statue and other objects hidden in a closet in his home."

"This can't be," Mrs. Hoag said. "He's been a good friend to me. Why would he do this? If he needed money, he had only to ask."

"Did Mr. Orr poison the birds?" Maureen asked.

"No, that was Jack and Al. They did all the breaking of the laws. They broke in here several nights, stealing art. It seems Mr. Hoag and Orr's father were boyhood friends and had used the secret tunnel many times. Although they swore never to tell a soul about the tunnel, Orr's father told him after Mr. Hoag's death when he was reminiscing about his friend. Sidney Orr figured he would use that knowledge."

"He wanted the land, didn't he?" Maureen said. She was feeling pleased with herself for figuring that out.

"Yes. He wanted to build houses here, but most of all he wanted to live in this mansion. If Mrs. Hoag died, everything went to charity. That wouldn't do him any good. But if he could scare her into leaving, he knew he could convince her to sell the house and the land to him. He had good artworks replaced by bad ones so she would think that she was imagining things and decide her mind was going and it wasn't wise to live here alone."

"What about Mrs. Hoag's handbag?" Mark asked. "Did the robbers throw it away?"

"Yes, they tossed it right after they came out of the tunnel, and it washed down to where you found it."

"I can't understand it," Mrs. Hoag said. "You think you know a person, and then he does something like this. Well, the excitement's over. Weren't we working in the Mexico Room?"

A week later Mrs. Hoag ushered Maureen and Mark into the Oriental Room for tea. Maureen knew immediately that she had something to say.

"I've been thinking," Mrs. Hoag started. "I've told you I wanted to open this house as a children's museum. But what about the land? I don't want houses close to the museum."

"We like to play at the creek," Mark said. "Maybe others would, too."

"It could be a park," Maureen suggested.

"That's it exactly," Mrs. Hoag said. "A park. And what would we put in a park?"

"Swings," Maureen said, "and other things to play on."

"Sidewalks," Mark said, "so people can walk down by the creek."

"Good ideas," Mrs. Hoag said. "We could put in some bird feeders, too, and let our feathered friends have a place to enjoy. I'm going to have my new lawyer draw up the papers. I'll get someone to design play things for the park and walking paths. Good, that's decided. Now, what will we name it?"

"Hoag Park," Maureen said.

"I thought of that, but it doesn't express what I want it to, although I'd like it to be in honor of Franklin, so he won't be forgotten. Would you like it to be in honor of someone?"

"Mama," Maureen whispered.

"Father," Mark said with a catch in his voice.

"Could we name it after all of them?" Mrs. Hoag said. "We'd need a fitting memorial. Oh. . .that'll be the name. Memorial Park."

By the Fourth of July the park was ready for a grand opening. Minneapolis dignitaries gathered around with townspeople of all ages for the unveiling of the name plaque.

When the band finished playing a rousing march, Mrs. Hoag, along with Mark and Maureen, climbed the steps of the large bandstand.

Once the applause died down, Mrs. Hoag said, "Today we come to dedicate this park to the memory of those we have loved and who have loved us—in particular to the memory of my husband, Franklin Hoag; to Maureen Stevenson's mama, Carleen O'Callaghan; and to Mark Bowman's father, Albert Bowman."

At her signal, Mark unveiled a large plaque that was set in the side of the bandstand.

"The inscription reads," she said, " 'To the memory of those who can no longer walk among us because they are walking in heaven. To those we have loved and lost, so that they may remain close to our hearts and minds, we dedicate this park, Memorial Park.' "

The crowd applauded and Maureen looked out at the large group. Mother and Father looked proud. Aunt Annie wiped away a tear.

"This is our gift to America," Mrs. Hoag said. "May God bless us all."